"One must imagine Sisyphus happy."

- Albert Camus

Chasing Your Tail

by Scott Taylor

720 Sixth Street, Unit #5
New Westminster, BC
V3L 3C5
CANADA

Title: Chasing Your Tail
Author: Scott Taylor
Publisher: Silver Bow Publishing
Cover Art: "Seagull Wheel of Dreams" painting by Candice James
Layout/Design: Candice James
Editing: Candice James

www.silverbowpublishing.com
info@silverbowpublishing.com
ISBN: 978-1-77403-277-0 paperback
ISBN: 978-1-77403-278-7 e- book
© Silver Bow Publishing 2023

Library and Archives Canada Cataloguing in Publication

Title: Chasing your tail / by Scott Taylor.
Names: Taylor, Scott (Author of Chasing your tail)
Identifiers: Canadiana (print) 20230556221 | Canadiana (ebook) 2023055623X | ISBN 9781774032770
   (softcover) | ISBN 9781774032787 (Kindle)
Subjects: LCGFT: Novels.
Classification: LCC PS3620.A946 C53 2023 | DDC 813/.6—dc23

Chasing Your Tail

1

I was going to Philly to visit Will. Will was my best friend, we'd gone to college together. He'd been living in Philly ever since we graduated, whereas me, I'd been living in Jersey my entire life (excepting the part where I went to college). I was Jersey, born and bred.

Will was waiting for me at the door when I got there. He had a tiny little apartment in a fairly sketchy part of town, where you could hear gunshots going off from time to time. It didn't seem to bother him too much but it bothered me plenty. I didn't want to get shot. Philly wasn't quite as bad as Newark, but it was pretty bad. I kept telling Will he needed to find a better place to stay but he never listened to me. Will was stubborn that way.

"C'mon, let's go get drunk," he said, already pushing his way out the door.

"Wait a minute, I just got here," I said.

"Doesn't matter," he said. Objection overruled.

We went out and hit the bars. That was pretty much the only thing we ever did, whether we were in Philly or in Jersey, it didn't matter. We weren't quite drunks yet but we were getting there. There was a neighborhood tavern type place around the corner where Will always took me and we went in there. Will knew the bartender, his name was Oleg. He was Polish. Oleg was actually a Russian name but he was Polish instead.

"Ahhhh, Will my friend, come in, come in," Oleg said, already setting up the shots of vodka and laying them down in a little line. He spoke with a heavy accent but it was easy enough to understand. He talked very slowly and his voice was extremely deep, as if coming up from the pits of hell.

"How's it goin' Oleg," said Will. We sat down and did the shots and followed them up with beers, then commenced to commiserate.

"So how's the writing going?" he asked me.

"Same as always. How's the music?"

"Same."

Will was a musician, I was a writer. That was the way it had been, ever since college. Neither one of us had gotten anywhere with it yet. It seemed to bother me more than it did him, although to be fair Will had always been a hard book to read. He had a million things going on in his head and none of them ever got out.

I started to say 'life's a bitch and then ya die,' then reconsidered; it was a dumbass thing to say. I rearranged my thoughts slightly.

"I don't know why you never seem to get frustrated like I do," I said instead, downing the rest of my beer and going for another.

"Sheer force of will. My spirit is indomitable."

Will was smart, he talked like that a lot. He was smarter than me. As I was searching for a response, the door opened and slammed behind us. Oleg growled.

"Ahhhh, here comes that damn Lithuanian. I can't stand that damn Lithuanian," he said.

The Lithuanian sidled up to the bar and ordered a drink. Oleg went grumbling to get it. No one had said the Lithuanian's name yet so I didn't know what it was. He remained nameless.

He had a big beer belly and wild unkempt hair and bloodshot eyes. Oleg brought the drink back over, slammed it down on the bar and they both just stood there looking at each other, having a staring contest, neither one willing to look away first. I looked inquiringly at Will.

"They know each other, they're like best friends," Will murmured over his shoulder. "It's like a routine, they do it every time."

It was a dive bar, an old man bar, the best kind. We sat for a while in silence, enjoying the ambience, soaking in the vibes.

"I love this place," I said at length.

"Best bar in Philly," Will said.

He ordered another round of shots, up and down they went. Will was getting more animated. I could still hold my liquor better than he could but he was catching up fast. I could tell he'd been practicing.

"Some nights I come in here and Oleg is lying there passed out on the bar," he said, leaning into me, snickering.

"On his own bar?" I said.

"Yep," said Will. "Face-first, right on the bar."

"How do you get drinks?"

"You don't."

"Best bar in Philly," I agreed. More shots were soon to follow.

We went to a few more places that night and then stumbled back to Will's place. In the morning we were both hungover, but not too bad. We'd had a hell of a lot worse, and not all that long ago either. I was still rubbing my eyes and clearing the cobwebs when Will came in from the bedroom, plucked the guitar off the stand and started to play. He sounded good. He sounded better each time I heard him, in fact. I knew he'd been practicing like a sonofabitch and it was really starting to come together. He was even writing his own stuff now.

"You're getting pretty good," I said.

"Thanks," he said.

"Had any gigs lately?"

"Yeah, a few. Mostly coffee shops, a coupla bars. The really small ones."

"You're gonna be famous before you know it. Gonna be a household name," I said.

Will was going to be famous before I was and I wasn't going to like it when it happened. I'd have to step up my own game, pick up the pace.

2

A few days later I was at work. The cube farm was so quiet you could hear a pin drop. The lights were sizzling down as always, broiling us in boredom. Greg came over.

"Listen man, we gotta get our asses in gear, the witch is pushing for that new code by end of day tomorrow. How're you making out?"

I wasn't making out at all, I'd barely even looked at it, but I didn't say that to Greg. I just kept staring.

"What the hell are you staring at?" Greg asked. "You're always staring into her office. She's not even that good-looking, and she's old, I mean what the hell are you thinking?"

I redirected my stare from the office to him.

"Why are you always coming over here to bother me?" I asked him. It was an honest question, one attempting to elicit an actual answer, but he just laughed it off instead.

"C'mon, it's lunchtime."

We went to the elevator, got in the elevator, rode the elevator down, got out and walked across to the cafeteria. I knew the way by now. Greg had taken the lead, as he always did, walking just in front of me with the same old bounce in his step he always had. It appeared Greg liked going to work. He wanted to be an 'architect', as in the computer version; that was supposedly the next step up the chain for guys like us. It was his mission in life to become an 'architect'. That, and have a great big family with seven or eight children and a big house to fill up with them. Greg had really gotten with the program lately. He'd already successfully completed the first step, which was to find the wife. The marriage had been about six months earlier, at a place out on Route 17, closer in towards the city, over by where my parents lived. I'd met his new wife only a few times, I didn't like her very much and the feeling was reciprocated. We were both just tolerating each other for Greg's sake, and for my part I wasn't sure why we were even doing that much as I didn't really like him either. I mean, he was okay, he was a friend of mine, but he bothered me a hell of a lot and sometimes I figured it was better just to stay home and watch TV or something. I was getting more and more like that in my old age.

We got our food and sat down.

"Seriously, do you have the hots for Christine?" he asked mid-munch.

"No," I said.

I was lying, I did. Christine was my boss. She was a couple of years older than I was, she was thin and slightly attractive with long black hair and pale white skin. She was also a bit of a wacko. That was understating it considerably, to be honest - she yelled and screamed all the time, all day long. With the hair and the pale skin and all, she looked something like a witch, which was rather apropos considering the circumstances. She had a few screws loose for sure. Everyone steered well clear of her for the most part, she'd throw these tantrums and they'd all just run for cover, but it didn't bother me at all, not in the slightest as a matter of fact. I had a thing for aggressive chicks, always had. It was kinda like my cross to bear, I guess you could say. Greg didn't know this about me and I wasn't about to tell him. Very few people knew.

"She's too old for you. That, and she's your friggin' boss. That, and she's a total bitch on top of it. There's a reason why she isn't married yet, you do realize that, don't you."

I didn't answer. Greg sat there with his patented quasi-manic bulbous-eyed stare, big teeth gleaming like daggers recently polished and filed. He looked like a shark. His eyes were always popping right out of his head and when he smiled it got even worse. One of these days he was going to get too excited and they were going to explode.

"Jeannie and I are going to the game on Sunday, wanna come?"

"Which game?"

"The Giants game."

Greg was a die-hard Giants fan, he'd told me about a thousand times but I always forgot. I wasn't into sports.

"No, thanks, I got stuff going on."

"You do not."

"No, I do, I gotta go see my folks. They invited me over for dinner."

"Looking forward to that, are you?" Smiling wide, looking More shark toothed than usual. He knew all about my parents.

"Yeah." End of conversation.

3

I went home that night and made dinner, a TV dinner thing I popped in the microwave. I ate a lot of frozen food in general, I ate pizza, I ate McDonalds, I wasn't going to last the week. I figured something was going to kill you, it might as well be your diet. That, and I had no idea how to cook, which probably had something to do with it as well.

After dinner, I sat down to write. Same spot as always, hunched over that flimsy little desk of mine, prepared to put some Immortal Words down on paper. The problem was, they never came. I'd been waiting for about three years for them to come and they never came. I figured I'd been through enough by now and it was high time to get started, high time for those Immortal Words to come pouring out of me like sweat, to go gushing like a veritable fountain of inspiration flooding first my room and then the world with the undeniable force of my burgeoning brilliance; but no dice, it just never seemed to happen. So many stories to write, so many things to say, so many words to use, so many goddamn combinations to try. The options were limitless. They were *too* limitless. There once was a cat, there once was a dog, there once was a frog that sat upon a log. There once was a woman who loved too much, there once was a man who knew too little, there once was a prince, there once was a prostitute, there once was a goddamnit it never ever worked. Three years of endlessly waiting, night after night spent propping up that stupid little desk in the corner, perched there like a monk in prayer, poised in penitent spiritual penury, waiting for the thunderbolt to strike, three years of silence, three years of ineptitude, thirty-six months of shame, one thousand ninety-five days of utter futility. It was enough to make you just throw in the towel and die. Will was going to get discovered soon and I'd be left behind, left there to eat his dust. The mere possibility of it rankled beyond bearing. It was success or bust, success or death. Failure not an option. Although I was currently swimming in it. God was testing me, yeah, that was it, he just wanted to see me suffer a bit first, wanted to watch me squirm, then once I'd paid my dues it would be clear sailing, all blue skies and sunshine for miles. It was just a matter of time, I knew that, I knew it deep down in the depths of my achy breaky heart. Soon the words would start flowing, soon the tales would start growing, soon my talent would be showing, soon the winds of change would be blowing. Someday my prince would come. But enough was enough, let him come soon. If he didn't, I was going to go out and find the sonofabitch and murder him in his sleep.

So it was more of the same that night, I sat there and did basically nothing. I typed up a few hundred words, that was it, really crappy stuff, unoriginal, boring as hell, it put me to sleep just to type it. I went to the fridge and got myself a beer, grumbled my disgruntled ass through it and packed myself off to bed. The calendar had turned another page, I was another day older and still nothing had happened. This was what finished guys like Van Gogh off, this was what put the shotgun in Papa Hemingway's mouth, this was what put the poets in their early graves.

4

I wasted Saturday doing nothing as well. The next day was Sunday. I had to go have dinner with my folks that night. I sat around all day just thinking about it, dwelling on the possible repercussions. Dealing with my folks oftentimes felt like a near-death experience, you got out of there wiping the sweat from your brow, feeling like you'd just barely made it out alive. Seven o' clock rolled around. Shit, time to go. There was no getting around it.

I got in the car and fought my way eastward, crawling down the highway, braving the angry urban hordes, the packs of wild animals trapped in their metal cages, ready to kill over an inch of space. Always a pleasure. It took almost an hour to go ten miles and then I was there. My father was waiting for me at the door.

"About time," he said.

My father was a smart ass. He thought the same of me, he'd told me so on numerous occasions. The difference was that he could get away with it because he had lots of money, whereas I did not, and therefore could not. You could run your mouth all you wanted when you had lots of money. My Dad had taught me that. Okay, the rest of the world had helped too. Anyway, there we were in the living room, my mother, my father and I. My brother Jake was still upstairs. Just being in the room with them was entirely nerve-rattling. The three of us squared off, preparing to do battle.

"So how are things going?" my father said, like it was an opening statement. They were sitting on the couch, I was sitting in the chair, the big armchair in the corner, the one right next to the grandfather clock.

"They're going okay," I said. I remained tense and nervous. Talking to my father always felt like some kind of interrogation.

"The job is still going all right?"

"Yep, it's all right."

I had a bottle of beer in my hand, which my Dad had just given me. Dad was drinking scotch and Mom was drinking wine. It was 'happy hour'. This was the hour when everyone had drinks together and pretended they were happy. Happy hour was a daily obligation, like some sort of staged performance we were all forced to take part in. We did it the same way every single time, no deviations possible, no ad-libbing of any kind. Switching any part of the routine would have been like committing a crime. Dad always drank the same scotch, in the same quantities, out of the same glass, and my mother did the same with her wine; the conversations were always the same, the topics never varied, the words that were used and the ways in which they were spoken were so predictable you could have written them out beforehand in a script. It was all so stuffy and formal and no one ever really appeared to be enjoying themselves, I didn't know why they even did it.

My mother sniffed the air dryly. "Are you still thinking about getting that new apartment?" she asked.

She didn't like the apartment I was in, it was a bit on the ratty side and she clearly didn't approve and enjoyed telling me all about it every chance she got. Everything was about money with my mother, always had been, always would be. She was more obsessed with money than my father was, which was saying a lot, something I always found funny considering the fact that it was really my Dad's money, he was the one who actually made it. He made the money, she figured out how to spend it. I was never getting married.

"Yes, I'm still thinking about it," I said. I wasn't, and never had been, I'd just said it to get her off my back.

"You need to get a better job, otherwise you'll never be able to afford anything better. I don't know why you took that horrible apartment in the first place."

I didn't respond to that one. It was just another argument waiting to happen and I wasn't going to take the bait. Anyway, the answer was obvious - one followed the other. A shitty job led to a shitty apartment, case closed. Not too hard to figure out really.

My Dad did some more talking and then Jake came downstairs. He dragged himself across the room and sat down in the opposite corner, shambling like some creature from the swamp. He looked about the same as always, which is to say not so good. Jake was depressed, had been since the beginning of time.

"How's the supermarket?" I asked from across the room, just for something to say.

"Okay," he said.

Jake worked in a supermarket, he bagged groceries, pushed the carts around for old ladies and things.

"Good to hear," I said.

No further response. That was all he was going to say, unless I made the effort to pull more out of him, and I wasn't prepared to make said effort and so that was that. We could all just sit there and look at the floor for all I cared.

About an hour later we were all sitting at the dining room table, eating our dinner. We were having steak, steak and potatoes to be exact, filet mignon and baked potatoes, to be even more exact. Steak was Dad's favorite, it was just about all he ate. Filet mignon and more filet mignon, filet mignon like there was no tomorrow. There was a social status associated with eating steak, primarily based on the fact that you could afford to buy it. I could tell it made him feel successful to eat it, privileged, elite, a member of the club. I sensed a conspiracy whenever we ate steak. Like I was a traitor to the common man. My Dad was one of those guys, you know the type, the ones who smoked cigars, played golf, followed the stock market. The country, the world and everything else made perfect sense to my father, he was the world's most contented human being. As such, he made absolutely no sense to me. I often wondered what the point of these little get-togethers was.

"You were talking about maybe getting a new car, too, weren't you Jim," my Dad said. Everyone was busy tucking in, knives and forks clinking, jowls flexing, mouths masticating. It was a regular feast.

"Nah, I think the old one is doing just fine," I said.

"It's as old as the hills," my mother said.

"It's five years old," I said. This is what I was talking about. What was the point.

"Jake here is getting a promotion," Mom said, pointing her hooded glare at her younger son, frowning at the hair all hanging in his eyes.

"It's not a promotion, it's a raise," Jake mumbled.

"Well, either way, we're very proud of him," Mom said. She patted his arm and went back to her food. My father remained noncommittal. Anything short of a corporate takeover was unlikely to produce much of a reaction.

I weathered the rest of the storm, parried my way through a few more uncomfortable minor disagreements and then was on my way. I worried a little about Jake on the way home, he really wasn't looking too good. But then again, he never did. Jake was an odd duck, he'd never fit in at school, didn't have any friends, wasn't too good with the ladies. That was actually an understatement - he'd never had a girlfriend in his life, which was a big part of the problem, I think. I was an odd duck myself but not on the same level as Jake, he took it to another place entirely. It was strange the way two perfectly well-adjusted parents could spawn such disaffected progeny. Maybe those theories on genetics were all just a bunch of horseshit.

5

Back at home, laying in bed. Not quite dreaming, but not quite awake, a state of semi-consciousness, dimly aware, darkly sentient. Tracey is making an appearance again. She shows up about once a week, usually when I'm at my lowest. It's the same sad scene, she's in her shorts and running shoes with her hair all wild and tousled and she's sitting on the couch watching me guardedly and she's made her decision already and I'm fighting the urge to kneel before her, right there at her feet, despite the fact it's all I want to do I'm fighting it with every fiber of my being. Sure it's what I want, but it's more than that, it's playing out on multiple levels now, I want to prostrate myself before her smug sated perfection, beg her to take me back, tell her I'll be good, I'll be better, I'll be whatever the hell she wants, but she just sits there and glares and says nothing, and I do nothing, I don't genuflect, I don't talk, I just watch. Everyone else is out, the apartment is empty, it's just her and I, no one else is there to witness whatever comes next. She's still the most beautiful thing I've ever seen, she is liquid feminine perfection, nothing else even comes close. She fills my chest up with molten lead. She's going off to med school soon, it's all she wants, all she cares about, she's only told me about a dozen times already. She raises her hand dismissively like Caesar and my head catches fire and there's bright bursting light and now I'm sliding down the tunnel again, same one as always, slipping and sliding and screaming my lungs out noiselessly no wind left and before I know it I'm at the bottom and Tracey isn't there anymore, which is good and bad, on the one hand it's nice because I don't have to watch her sitting there disapproving anymore but on the other it's horrible because I can't stand to be parted from her no matter what she's doing to me. I've been dumped out into the parking lot of the apartment complex, that ski chalet place, lying there on the asphalt sprawling all over the place with the cars going by just a few feet away. Up the big steep hill, the campus looms overhead. It's mid Spring, April or so, there's still some snow on the ground and the icicles are still clinging to the eaves but we're only a few weeks away from graduation. Crazy ass northern Springs. About six weeks away from the end, the end of all things as we know them. In six weeks she'll go away and so will they and so will I, and all that will remain are these goddamn flashing images that will go on haunting me from now until the end of time. I wish I'd never gone at all.

In the morning I'm better though, I barely remember what happened. I usually recover quickly, I guess I'm resilient that way. I go and make coffee, put some bread in the toaster, have a bite to eat. Another day on planet Earth. More present melting into past. What a sorry state of affairs. The weather is nice, perhaps I'll go for a walk. A walk in the lovely morning sunshine, that's the ticket, who could say no to that. Maybe I'll go to the movies, I haven't done that in a while.

6

I was hanging out with Jake. We'd made plans to get together the night I'd gone over there for dinner. I'd offered to go pick him up and bring him over to Morristown but he refused, saying he'd take the bus instead. Typical Jake, he'd do shit like that just to spite you, just to spite himself, even if it was easier for him to just go with the flow. We'd never exactly been buddies in the past, but I was making more of an effort to get to know him now. He was weird but he was interesting. Part curiosity, part familial duty. My mother had been encouraging it all along and I was finally in the mood to humor her.

We were strolling in the park, the little town square with its ring of shops and eateries and things.

"Feel like going to a bar?" I asked him.

"Nah," he said.

"Well what you wanna do then?"

"Dunno."

"Come on, Jake, give me some ideas."

"Don't bust my balls, I don't know."

I thought about insisting on the bar but then reconsidered, I didn't want to make him mad. Jake could get scary when he was mad, it didn't happen often but when it did he went positively psycho and you had to clear out of there or you were dead. We passed a bench and for lack of better options we sat on it.

"So how's life?" I asked. He glared at me distastefully, I grinned back at him like a lunatic.

"You sound like Dad," he said.

"I know," I said. I wasn't exactly trying to piss him off but the idea had crossed my mind.

"Life is fine, Jim."

"No it isn't." It was working, he was getting pissed off.

"No, come on, tell me what's going on. You don't look too happy."

"Dude, I work in a friggin' supermarket. I live with my parents. What do you want from me."

It was almost five, getting close to rush hour. Across the way two cars almost got in an accident, both guys leaning on the horn simultaneously, followed by a whole lot of yelling and screaming, the two of them leaning out the window prepared to do murder. Jersey stuff, just business as usual.

"It's not that bad. Life's what you make it, and all that," I said dismissively, trying to mask the fact that I knew full well what he meant. If you were talking to someone who was regularly depressed, and you were regularly depressed yourself, the last thing in the world you wanted to say was 'I agree with you.' I started telling Jake about smelling the roses and about how pleasant life could be if you just learned to roll with the punches a little and the more I did it the more I sounded like that father of mine, so I stopped. Jake looked relieved.

"Look, spare me the bullshit. I know you don't even mean any of the things you just said."

"Some of them, I do. Depends on my mood." I was grinning again, trying to cheer him up, but he was back to looking gloomy as all hell and so once again I stopped.

"Wanna walk around some more?" I asked him.

"Not really," he said.

"And I'm the one busting *your* balls. Come on, we'll go back and watch some TV. There's gotta be something on."

"How thrilling."

We went back and watched TV, got some fast food takeout and then Jake went home. For the rest of the night I sat there thinking about him. The kid looked down, he was definitely not right. The whole loner thing was bad enough when you were back in school, but it got about ten times worse once you got out, once the dress rehearsal was over and you had to try to deal with it in real life. There were few places for lone wolves to hide. Jake needed a hobby, he needed something to do with his life. He'd been talking about trying to play guitar for years now, maybe I'd start encouraging him to do that. Not that he'd ever listen to me in a million years. That kid would never listen to anyone, he'd rather die first. My brother was one pissed off dude.

7

I was back at work. It felt like I was there more than I was anywhere else. Probably because it was true. Christine had called me in for a little talk. It had given me a thrill just to walk in there, a little jolt of electrical juice shooting down my spine as I went into the office and closed the door behind me.

I sat down in the chair and faced her. She stared at me coolly, levelly, with just a hint of a smirk playing at the corners of her mouth. I was cowed, it was hard meeting her gaze.

"So, I have to ask you, Jim - what time do you come in to work in the morning?" She was trying to behave herself for a change, trying to be civil.

"Oh, around 9:45," I said.

I was lying, it was always ten or later, every single time, I didn't give a shit about being late and I didn't give a shit about losing my job either. You could say I just didn't give a shit.

"Okay, let's make sure it isn't any later than that though."

I was being let off with a warning. That was it, she dismissed me and I went back to my box. I'd been hoping for more, with that little smirk of hers and all.

Off in the corner, over by the water cooler, Greg was having a chat with Relative Ed. We called him Relative Ed because he was always saying 'everything is relative.' He seemed to say it whenever he couldn't think of anything else to say. Sometimes it made sense given the context of the conversation and sometimes it didn't. Anyway, that was what we called him. Relative Ed spoke painfully slowly, like in a drawl but without any of the southern inflection or hillbilly whine. He wasn't a hick or anything, he'd grown up somewhere nearby but for some reason he spoke like there was something wrong with him, I couldn't figure it out. He spoke so slowly that you never made it to the end without just giving up and tuning him out completely. He was one of these invisible men who was never listened to by anybody, who passed through life like some sort of ghost. All day long he sat there doing his coding and whenever he tried to speak everyone just drowned him out. It was kind of sad really. Relative Ed was about the same age as Greg and I but he looked quite a bit older. He wasn't aging well. Then again, I don't think he'd looked too good to begin with. He was prematurely bald and had a big paunch and a mustache that didn't seem to fit in with anything else on his face. He had some sort of large potted plant in his cube that took up more room than he did. He said it was a 'corn plant'. He said he had two more just like it back at home.

I went over to join them.

"So how did it go?" Greg asked me.

"She told me to stop coming in late."

"Did you get your rocks off?"

"Shut up, you moron."

I had no idea if Greg had told Relative Ed about the thing I had for Christine, and I didn't really care. Like everyone else I had trouble recognizing his existence, it was almost like he wasn't even there. Relative Ed was in the process of trying to balance a newly-poured cupful of water along with the styrofoam cup of coffee he'd already acquired earlier and it wasn't going so well, he was about to spill both of them all over the floor. He was also a total klutz, I forgot to mention that part.

His cube was about ten feet away, all he had to do was go over and drop the friggin' coffee off there first and then come back but it was obviously much easier to stand there juggling everything around and flirting with disaster the whole time. People were brain dead.

"Ed wants to go out with us on Friday night," Greg said. It sounded like a threat.

"I didn't know we were going out," I countered.

"You did so, you said yesterday we were going to Lido's."

"I can't, I'm going to Philly to see Will."

"Again?"

"Yes, again."

"You should just move there, you're there so much."

Pause. Tired of answering his bullshit.

"Okay, next Friday then."

"Sounds good."

I looked at Relative Ed to check for a reaction, saw nothing written on his face whatsoever, just a big round white moon hovering there in space, a clean slate full of nothing. Relative Ed was a goddamn weirdo, I didn't know why Greg had set this whole thing up. I wasn't exactly looking forward to next Friday night.

I went home and dreamt of Christine. I thought about what it would have been like just to get down there and shine her shoes for her. She was such a bitch she probably would have enjoyed it, and yet it never seemed possible to do anything like that. There was this whole big huge world out there and there wasn't the slightest thing you could do with it. There were about five things you were allowed to do; you could go to work, come home, eat meals, sleep, pay your bills, that was about it. Every six months you could go lay down on a beach. It was like we were all locked into riding along on these tracks and no one ever made any effort whatsoever to jump them. The whole thing just seemed like a waste of time. The only other person in my life who seemed to notice any of this was Will. Which was probably why I spent so much time in Philly. Will and I were going to start a revolution one day, we'd talked about it, it was only a matter of time. He'd sing the songs and I'd write the books and soon the whole world would be seeing things our way. It was written in the stars, it was nothing short of destiny. All one of us had to do was make it first. And goddamnit, it was going to be me. I wasn't going to be left eating his dust.

8

I was in Philly, visiting Will. Visions of Christine were still dancing in my head, she was a hard bitch to forget about. Then again, I'd always had trouble dislodging chicks from my brain, ever since high school in fact. But Christine was in there good, she'd established quite a stranglehold and was determined not to let go. I told Will about it.

"There's something about her, man. She's got this hard bossy streak that drives me nuts."

"Well, she *is* your boss."

"Yeah, but they're not all like that. Some of them are actually nice."

"Roll with it then. See what happens."

"I can't. There's no chance of anything actually happening. It's not sustainable."

"Sustainable again." It was a word I overused, rather badly at times. I was turning into Relative Ed and I hadn't even noticed it.

We drank some more. "She's got ya good, eh?" Will said.

"Yeah. She's got my number man. She talks down to me, tells me what to do, looks at me like I'm a bug."

"Waiting to be squashed." Will smacked his lips dramatically, lasciviously. He knew all about my various mental and sexual oddities. I would have trusted Will with my life. He was a mate, the best kind. Like a brother really.

We'd walked into the first bar we came to, it was even divier than our usual. It was a tiny little closet of a place with a sad-looking pool table up on a riser in back. The walls and floors were like cardboard and the whole thing looked like it was ready to collapse in on itself. Two big drunk guys were having an argument right next to us at the bar, two huge hulking working-class brutes, salt of the earth types under normal circumstances only they'd managed to rile each other up on this particular occasion. We took our beers and went up on the riser to shoot some pool. Suddenly the noise was escalating, I looked over just in time to see the one guy drop the other one with a punch in the face; there was a sickening thud and then he went over like a ton of bricks, fell like a sack of potatoes, hit the ground like a Mack truck running into a brick wall. He was a seriously big dude. The bartender was bellowing now and so the guy who was still standing got out of there fast - at least as fast as a big drunk galoot like him could move.

"Jesus Christ, the first bar we go into," I said.

"The portents be not propitious," Will said, screwing around. Like I said, I was the writer and Will was the musician but he was damn smart, and there was some crossover there as well, he did a little writing on the side and I played some guitar. Or at least had in a past life, it had been a few years now since I'd even looked at one.

"C'mon, let's get outta here," I said. "This place is depressing."

We got out of there and went down the block. It was cold and windy but a hell of a lot better than it had been the week before. Spring was just around the corner. Will was moving along in his usual striding fashion, each stride of epic length, covering about ten feet per step; it was like watching a tree falling forward over and over again, a silent measured crashing, the same rhythm every time. Will was about six-four, he may have even been six-five, I couldn't remember what he'd told me. He was thin and had a scraggly brown beard, he looked a bit like a stretched-out Jesus. A gumby Messiah.

"I've got a new girl, did I mention that?" Will said.

"No! How could you not have mentioned that already? What's her name?"

"Priti. She said she was going to meet us out tonight."

"Outstanding."

Will had had a rough start with the ladies back in college but he'd rebounded nicely afterwards. Now every time I talked to him he had a new iron in the fire, or two, or three. I was damn proud of him. Me, I was going the other direction, I'd had some limited success in college but now had contracted leprosy or something and the chicks wouldn't come within fifty feet of me. Life was a bitch, how else could you put it. Or a series of them. Some days were lemons and so you made lemonade, but when lemonade was all you were drinking the experience became a fair bit stale. I'd been drinking so much lemonade lately my lips were almost permanently shriveled shut, like somebody's puckered little asshole.

Anyway, so now I was looking forward to meeting Will's new girl. He had good taste in women and they were always interesting as hell, if nothing else. There was another place where we were supposed to be meeting her and so we went there. It was on the other side of town, we took the bus.

This second bar was a lot nicer, more upscale. Normally Will and I wouldn't have given this type of joint the time of day but he was obviously trying to show off for the new girl and I was willing to play along. We waited awhile and then there she was. She was a rail-thin Indian chick, quite attractive, with dark features and big round almond eyes. She was just about all eyes in fact. She sat down next to me in the booth and we shook hands.

"Hi, I'm Priti."

"Jim. Nice to meetcha."

We chatted for a few minutes, just feeling each other out, getting the lay of the land. She had the same sort of drugged look that Will always had, perhaps that was what had drawn the two of them together. Well, maybe not drugged, but she was mellow to the point of sleep. Mellow was good, mellow worked for me. She was doing the same thing he always did which was to avoid eye contact and let her gaze go drifting around the room instead, even while she was talking; it was spooky, it was like watching a female version of him. Perhaps she'd been spending too much time with him already and was starting to pick up all his quirks. They said people did that with their dogs as well.

"So where did you guys meet?" I asked her.

"Online," she said.

"Online is a scary place," I said.

"It seriously is," she said. "But that's where I found this crazy guy, so I guess it was worth it in the end."

I turned to Will. "I can't believe you hadn't mentioned it yet, that you were dating someone new..."

"Hadn't gotten around to it yet," he said, downing a beer.

"Will is off in his own world," Priti said.

"Permanently."

"But in a good way."

"Agreed."

It was a wonderful thing whenever one of Will's new chicks got around to appreciating him like this. If anyone deserved it, it was Will. He really had had a rough start.

"So what do you do for a living?" I asked her.

"I'm a doctor," she said.

"A doctor? No shit," I said, with raised eyebrow. I hadn't been expecting the response. The plot thickened. This one probably had some horsepower up above the shoulders. Another point in her favor. Like that McCartney dude said, 'maybe another kind of mind there...' The portents had repositioned themselves, the evening now had a degree of promise.

We ordered another round of beers. Priti was a lightweight, she was already starting to get a little buzzed. The conversation veered all over the place, the three of us were just babbling, talking to fill up space and time. Will had been going on about how Priti was a 'neurotic' and I could see what he meant; her movements and speech were all flighty and herky-jerky and half the time she appeared spooked by things that weren't there. Then suddenly her eyes got real wide and before I knew what was happening she was slipping down under the table, sliding down on her back as if easing herself into water, going all the way under and disappearing completely from view. I looked over at Will and he didn't seem to mind, in fact he looked like he'd barely noticed. I couldn't tell if she was having a panic attack and trying to get out of the line of fire, or if she was about to give me a blowjob. I waited to feel hands on my zipper but there were no gropings there and then a few seconds later Priti reappeared on the bench as if nothing had happened. I was all for spontaneity and unconventional behavior but this was downright weird. I mean give me a clue what's going on.

We left the bar and took a long leisurely walk. Will was a real city type, he didn't mind walking long distances cross town and his girls never did either. He prided himself on knowing the bus routes backwards and forwards. It came from not having a car. He'd had a car and a license and all that at one time but he'd gotten in an accident (ironically enough with a bus) and hadn't driven since. I considered myself to be in pretty good shape but I always had trouble keeping up with him whenever we went on walkabout like this.

We came to a Polish bar and went inside for another drink. You could tell it was a Polish bar by the beer sign hanging outside the door. The scene inside was frenzied. The place was full of locals, Polacks of all different shapes and sizes, and they were drinkin' and hootin' and hollerin' with abandon, really whooping it up, it felt more like some lowbrow European festival than a night out at the bar. Will really knew how to find these places. They were playing some crazy Polish music on the jukebox and the bartender was speaking Polish with the barflies lined up at the bar and the night started to swim and everyone was having a grand old time, and I looked at Priti and she didn't seem fazed in the slightest by anything at all and neither did Will and so I decided I wasn't either. There were no Lithuanians here. Will and I went in the back and shot a few games of pool and Priti just watched. Someone had gotten sick somewhere back in the deep dark recesses of the place and a faint odor of vomit was discernible. The smell of it was getting to me a little but once again the others didn't seem to mind and so I pretended not to notice. The jukebox started playing a polka and a couple of the old-timers got up to dance, followed by a young feller who was drunker than the rest, who asked for one of the maiden's hands and was accepted. Will and I went up to the bar for more beer and now the barflies were offering us shots of vodka and of course we had to say yes. The room was now spinning a little. The rest of the night quickly became a blur and the next thing I remembered was waking up in the morning on Will's floor. Priti wasn't there, she'd evidently gone home at some point. Will came out and picked up the guitar, started strumming.

"So what did you think of her?"

"She's nice. She's quirky."

"Quirky is the only way to go."

Once again, Will was right. He was right most of the time. Maybe even all the time. Will was one of my heroes. Heroes were in short supply for me these days, but he was definitely one of them.

9

The night had come when we were supposed to be going out with Relative Ed. I really didn't want to go, but I didn't want to be rude and bail either. At about five-thirty we took separate cars over to Lido's. Lido's was the local watering hole, the spot where people went for drinks after work. A corporate place full of corporate stiffs. It was Friday night and the bar was chock full of people, fellow cubicle denizens like ourselves mostly. I even recognized a few of them. It was standing room only at first, but then we squeezed in at the bar when another little group left. We ordered drinks. Greg was in the middle, with Relative Ed on one side and me on the other. I'd arranged it this way on purpose so that (hopefully) I wouldn't have to talk to Relative Ed too much. He was already endlessly droning on about something and Greg was in the process of trying not to ignore him. I didn't know why he bothered, it was a lost cause. I leaned in close.

"Why did you agree to this?" I whispered.

"He asked. And I felt sorry for him. No, actually he isn't that bad once you get to know him." I remained skeptical. Greg turned back to face the other way.

"So, Ed, how are the plants at home doing?"

I could tell he didn't really know what else to ask him. He'd picked the right subject though - Relative Ed stiffened with pride, gathering himself, preparing to discourse at length.

"They are beginning to thrive, after a long period of relative adversity. I am still trying to understand exactly how much sunlight they require, as well as how much water, and also whereabouts in the house they would prefer to sit, the location that would best suit them. I am also considering purchasing one or two more of these plants, to fill another space which is currently left vacant in the corner, closer in towards the dining room. It is a location that could prove inconvenient, however, as it is also closer to the main hallway and could conceivably interfere with the comings and goings of any visitors who might be passing through the area. I have yet to decide whether or not to proceed with the proposed expansion."

"Logistical problems," observed Greg.

"Foot traffic, and all," I added.

I was surprised I'd made it through to the end. His words absolutely flowed like sludge, it was like torture to listen to, it all but damaged your ears to hear it, and he spoke in such a strange, stilted way, like some foreigner or something. He was a serious weirdo, a real strange brew. He also didn't look particularly comfortable being out and about, his bald pate was shining with sweat and he was beginning to fumble over his speech a bit. The guy next to him on the other side had leaned in and gotten a little too close at one point and you could see him physically shrinking, drawing away as if expecting a blow. I don't think Relative Ed got out very much. He was probably at least half a shut-in, you know, one of these people who goes from home to work to home again and little else. Someone who has trouble going out and getting groceries at the store. Good thing they delivered these days.

"Yes," he said.

"Weren't you saying that last year the plants were on the verge of death?" Greg said.

"They were, yes, you are correct Greg, you have an excellent memory, an excellent memory indeed. I have noticed this about you many times in the past. The plants were in fact not doing well at this same time last year. I was never able to pinpoint the exact cause, but I was led to believe it may have been due to overwatering. The online reviews of the text I'd been following were speaking to the fact that there were possible faults in the instructions in this regard."

"So things could be worse," I added.

"I am sorry, Jim? I do not follow."

"Well, I mean, you were saying there'd been this period of difficulty. This year. But I suppose that's better than being on the verge of death. Last year. So things have improved."

"Yes, you are correct, Jim. Everything is relative."

It was the first time he'd said it that night. He'd said it twice earlier in the afternoon, however. Greg and I had a pool going on how often he said it daily, with an over/under and all.

The evening wore on, the pontifications continued without abatement. So many people out there seemed to enjoy hearing the sound of their own voices, I didn't know why they had to do that, didn't see what was to be gained from it. You certainly didn't learn anything new. I leaned back and let Greg continue with the conversation, figuring he could carry the load for awhile. I wasn't sure how long I was going to last. People like this tired me out severely, within minutes I was at the point of wanting to throw things. Then again, people did that to me in general, whether they were talking like mental patients or not. I wasn't exactly a 'people person'. It ran in the family, to an extent, my parents were sociable enough I supposed but my brother sure as hell wasn't.

I spaced out for a few minutes and looked around the room and when I returned to the discussion things were the same as before. I'd been vaguely aware of Greg trying to change the subject at one point, he'd been trying to steer

Relative Ed towards talking about his family (they were originally from Turkey, his great grandfather had been a sultan or something) but he'd quickly redirected it back to the plants. My Lord, the lives some people led. I waved to the bartender to get the tab.

"Where the hell are you going?" Greg asked. A minute ago he'd been reveling in my discomfort and now he was practically irate.

"Home," I said.

"Whaddya mean, home? We just got here."

"I know that."

"You've got nothing to do at home either and you know it, you're going to be bored either way."

"Everything is relative."

"Come on, don't leave yet, we just got here."

I thought about trying to come up with some excuse but then suddenly didn't find it necessary. Greg knew damn well what was going on, and on top of that he'd been the cause of the problem in the first place. He could go to hell if he didn't like it. I'd had enough, that was all I could handle, I couldn't handle no more. I paid the bill, said goodnight to Relative Ed and skedaddled. He barely even noticed I was leaving, he was in the middle of another big announcement. This was the last time I went out with him. I wasn't putting myself through this again, I'd rather go play in traffic.

10

I was still trying to write my big novel. Still wrestling with those Immortal Words, the ones that would never come. I'd sat down at the desk one night with a pot of coffee and a headful of ambition, practically sweating in advance, ready to duke it out all night long if need be, ready to make my final stand. This was it, it was time, it was Waterloo, it was Custer and the Indians, I wasn't prepared to wait any longer. It was now or never. I sat there for an hour, and still nothing, no dice, no luck, no goddamn words of any kind. At least none of the ones that mattered. They were in there but I couldn't figure out a way to get them out. There were flowers in my mind, daisies and lilies and starbursts all red and gold ready to flare into light, there was joy and mirth and tragedy, entire lives lived or waiting to be lived, a thousand galaxies wrapped up in a million multiverses. There were messages of truth and inspiration the world needed to hear, little shreds of enlightenment capable of buoying the human race for decades to come, maybe centuries even. There was treasure in the box but the key had been lost a long time ago and chances were I'd never find it again. I'd been writing some good shit back in school at one point but those days were long past, the spring had dried up, the light had been extinguished. And yet still I persisted. I didn't know when to quit. I was just as stubborn as Will, maybe even worse. This was going to drive me nuts if I kept at it too long, drive me clear over the edge, I could feel it.

I sat there for another hour. I could actually hear crickets chirping outside. The gods were laughing at me, they were out of earshot but I could sense their celestial cackles. I got up and paced around the room. Back and forth, back and forth. This having no appreciable effect, I went into the living room, picked up a book, sat down in the chair and started to read, but I couldn't manage to do this either. I couldn't concentrate, there were little buzzings and hummings and whinings in my head and I had to keep reading the same goddamn sentence three times before anything sank in. It was no use. I'd had anxiety my entire life but it was worse now, way worse. The writing problems certainly weren't helping matters any but that wasn't the whole story, not by a long shot. The whole story was that I was a basket case just like my brother and always had been. Sometimes I wondered what kind of mental illness ran in our family, what kind of wackos we'd had for ancestors; I pictured a whole gallery of nuts and con-men and serial killers and whatnot, a who's who of degenerates and maniacs, all in a little line, their demented faces leering from portraits in a hall. I mean, consider what was going on in my head - I was anxious to start with, which led me to the point where I couldn't read, which made me even more anxious that I couldn't read which made everything worse and it went round and round in circles forever. I was anxious about being anxious, I mean what the hell could you do with someone like that. I was disturbed, I needed heavy meds, I needed a lobotomy. I needed a vacation if nothing else, that much was for sure. A break from it all. A nice long vacation, somewhere hot and sunny. I didn't like beaches though, I differed from the rest of the family there. My parents just wanted to go pitch themselves in the sand somewhere and bake for weeks on end; that, to me, seemed like the essence of madness, to say nothing of being rather uncomfortable. I didn't see how it was possible to enjoy oneself whilst being cooked to a crisp. No, for me, it was hot and sunny but with air-conditioning and cold beer, a nice cool perch from which to witness all the hot sunny things taking place just beyond. Hmmm. California, Mexico. Spain. The Costa del Sol. One of these days I was going to get my ass in gear and just go, just pack a bag and run off and not come back for a year. Ten years, twenty years, hell, the rest of my life. Nothing but hot sunny places and random encounters and wild experiences henceforth, from now until the end of time. That would work just fine for me. The novel could go throw itself off a bridge. I didn't need that shit in my life anyway, all it did was bring me down. And I was down enough already.

11

Back at work, I sat in my box. There was no end to it, it was just going to go on like this until I died. I envisioned a skeleton in a chair, gathering dust, all but unnoticed, of no concern to anyone passing by. Unbeknownst to the others, I'd begun writing poetry there in the cubicle to pass the time and also to vent a little. I was supposed to be doing work but once again I didn't give a shit. There weren't too many people coming round so I could pretty much get away with it, although there were a few close calls here and there, someone popping in midstream and a whole lot of frantic shuffling of papers and clearing of throats. Greg had done it a couple of times already and I could tell he was beginning to suspect. Anyway, the poetry I was writing was real angry stuff, not like the usual flowery crap, half insane, almost nonsensical, lashing out at the cube and the office and the city and the country and the world, in roughly that order. I would scribble away in frenzied bursts and then read it back and marvel at how mad it all sounded. I doubted anyone else had ever sat in a cubicle writing angry poems before. I didn't know whether they should give me a prize or have me committed. I felt like I was losing my mind.

I had just finished another one when Christine came by, she was gathering everyone up for a powwow, a little chinwag in the conference room. Everyone got up and we went over. Christine seated herself at the end of the long table. She started talking. I had no idea what she was talking about because all I could do was fantasize about all the things she might do to me were she to drop the nice girl act and let loose with one of her patented torrents of abuse. I pictured her with a whip in her hand, standing over me menacingly, black eyes flashing, little red horns sprouting from her glistening brow. I wondered if she ever wore high heels. When I returned from space she was starting to get worked up about something. My dream was becoming reality.

"So why isn't it done?" she was asking Clark, one of the junior guys, a kid fresh out of college.

"Well, I've been having a bit of trouble with one of the modules," Clark replied sheepishly, looking down.

"Well, we need it done. It was supposed to have been done two weeks ago. You can always stay late or work on the weekends if you have to." She was fighting for control, you could see it, and little by little she was losing the battle. I held my breath. Another few minutes of this and she'd have me drooling on the carpet.

"So, in other business - the error log has been growing too. Nick, I thought I told you to let me know when we were getting close to the threshold. Remember the discussion last week about delegating the work when it got too high?"

"The system has been down quite a bit," Nick said. Nick was another one like me, he didn't care, he wasn't taking any crap from anybody. He was some kind of ex-biker dude or something, he wore his leather jacket into work and smoked a lot of cigarettes.

"I don't care about the system being down. I care about those reports going back to Richard."

Richard was Christine's boss, he was the big chief. It made her even more tense just to mention his name. "So you'll let me know when the queue is back down under twenty?"

Nick nodded perfunctorily. She wasn't quite browbeating him but it was getting close. I cast a hardened eye upon Nick, watching him like a jealous spouse. Sometimes I wanted to do things wrong just to push her buttons. Maybe she'd finally get the hint. We went back to our cubes and then one of the other managers went into Christine's office to have a chat. The door was closed and then I began to hear shouts, Christine had had enough, the dams had finally burst. And to think I'd only missed it by a few minutes. My timing had always been horrible. I thought about going to the keyhole to have a peep but figured that might be a touch too obvious. I'd never hear the end of it from Greg.

Greg came over. He was staring again, smiling with those eyes popping out; it made me nervous. "Tara wants to have dinner on Thursday night." Tara was his new wife. I assumed that meant she wanted me to come. I had no idea why.

"Yeah, sure," I said, with a note of trepidation that appeared to go undetected.

"Cool, I'll let her know."

Now what the hell was this all about. The last time I'd seen her she'd looked ready to kill me. Maybe she was going to get me drunk and then stab me after dessert. The way things were going I was liable to just let her do it.

12

Lying in bed with the dreams washing over me again. A deluge of memory, pouring like rain all over my face and eyes. It's nicer this time though, all about the good times at the beginning of college, before I got together with Tracey and everything went off the cliff. Less like rain, really, more like soaking in a nice warm bath. It's the Arts Quad in springtime and everything is nice and green and peaceful, with elegant buildings all around and trees in full bloom and all the little paths zigzagging back and forth and all the kids scurrying around in the throes of youth. I'm one of them, I feel great, I feel wonderful. I feel like sunshine. I'm sitting in the grass with a couple of friends with the libraries just off in the distance, looking like castles with their little stone turrets; off to the side the big slope leads down to West Campus and the city and the lake and the rest of the world there reveling in all its wondrous spring majesty, all green and blue and gold, pure, just waiting to be discovered. Pure, like us. The air is alive with sound, gentle rustlings, random tinklings, snippets of idle conversation scattered on the breeze. I'm being drowned in sweetness. My breathless youth blows hushed through the trees and I'm caught in a dream so pleasant I never want to wake up again, I just want to stay there, forever, never wake up again, not ever, not until the end of time and not even then. The happy times are always so fleeting, why do they have to run off like that. I'd been truly happy there for awhile, lost in my little world there at school with my whole life in front of me. At least for the first few years. Our eyes had been shining and there'd been a spring in our step and then in the blink of an eye we barely recognized each other anymore and it was time to move on, and we did, we moved on and the void swept in and replaced everything that had been good, everything that had ever meant anything at all. A hint of promise, followed by a massive crushing defeat so overwhelmingly final you couldn't even remember who you were anymore, or who you'd been. What was the point of the path if this was the place it led to. It just made no sense, and never had.

I woke up with sweat all over my face. I went into the bathroom to wash it off and then lay down again, but I couldn't go back to sleep no matter how hard I tried. It was going to be one of those nights, lying on my back just staring at the ceiling, waiting for dawn. I was well familiar with the experience. The visions were still there before my eyes and they wouldn't go away. Even the good memories eventually began to haunt you. In the end, it was all pain and sorrow, all that was left was the knowledge of what you'd lost.

The dream had me feeling nostalgic and so the next time I sat down to write (which was the following night) I started writing a little short story about college. I threw everything I had into it, the people I'd known, the places I'd gone, the way I'd felt, all the stories I could remember, all about sweet innocent Cathy and lovely Marie and crazy wacky George with his thousand and one quirks and peccadilloes and Will of course with all the things he was and a whole slew of other characters, minor acquaintances, people I'd been familiar with but hadn't known well enough, each of them so intriguing and endearing in their own little ways, and in the end it turned out pretty good, pretty damn good in fact, I thought. Maybe this was it, maybe I'd finally turned the corner, maybe the dam had burst. I'd only been waiting about a hundred years. I printed the story out and put it in a drawer, just to have a copy saved. I was on my way.

But a few more nights of frustration and I was back at square one. No dams had burst, no flood gates had been opened. It appeared to have been just a flash in the pan. Goddamn it. If my head was so filled to the brim with ideas, why couldn't I get any of them out. I'd tried getting drunk first, tried writing when excited, writing when tired, when angry, when sad, and none of it made a dent. My head was like a fortress, inaccessible even to me. Nothing worked. I came at it from the left, from the right, tried frontal assaults, tried outflanking it, tried everything I could think of and the defenses always held, the walls stood fast. Maybe I could try hypnosis, that might do the trick. Or hardcore drugs. LSD? Probably too dangerous. Forget writing, I'd never be able to speak properly again. Syd Barrett sitting in his parents' basement for the rest of eternity, no not for me, thank you very much. But I'd have to figure something out, I couldn't just sit here like this letting life pass me by. I should have been published by now, should have been a known quantity, making the rounds, doing productive work, getting out in the thick of it all. Meanwhile Will was going to get discovered, I could feel it, it was close. God damn it. What to do, what to do. I went into the other room and got a beer, had two, had three, sat there at the kitchen table and steamed. It seemed to me like the world was meant for certain people and not others, like it had been earmarked for a select few, right from the beginning, and no amount of effort or complaining or thrashing about was ever going to make the slightest iota of difference. Like God had a guest list and I wasn't on it. Saint Peter, the universal bouncer. Conspiracies abounded, it wasn't just with writing, it was with everything, it was total. Everywhere you went you were running into walls or there was some door slamming in your face. I didn't know why we bothered if the cards were all stacked like that, why we dressed and fed ourselves, why we even got up in the morning. It was much easier just to lie in bed anyway. Maybe I'd just start doing that instead.

13

It was time to have dinner with Greg and his wife. I wasn't ready for it but once again I had to go. Like I said, I didn't mind Greg too much but this new wife of his really gave me the creeps, it was like talking to a vaguely hostile mannequin. I went over at the appointed hour, they let me in through the door and we sat down in the living room. The sensation was eerily similar to the one felt upon entering my parents' living room. Drinks were procured, the mannequin said a few socially required words and then went off to tend to dinner. Greg took me into his den to show me some stuff he had in there, some trophies he'd won back in high school, some pictures hanging on the wall. It was supposed to be male bonding of some sort, I supposed, but all we were really doing was killing time. The old sense of futility - why didn't we just stay in our own homes and dispense with all the bullshit. Why had she wanted to have me over anyway. 'Propriety', Tolstoy would have said. He'd been slinging that word around a lot in the book I'd been reading lately.

So there was a fair bit more propriety, a few more drinks drunk and then finally we sat down to dinner. The tablecloth was nice and clean, the silverware all silvery shiny. Music was on in the background, pleasant soothing sounds, practically sleep-inducing. Sounded like the stuff my mother used to play when we were kids. That Lite FM station. Tara sat at the head of the table, stiff and erect, surveying the scene, perceiving me dimly. She wore the pants in the family, I could tell. That didn't surprise me in the slightest considering how hard I'd watch Greg fall for her, they used that shit against you once they knew you were hooked. She started off the proceedings herself.

"So, Jim, Greg says you're writing a book?"

"Yes, I've been working on a novel for quite some time now."

Something about the way she spoke to me always made me respond in a manner that was far too formal; I'd tried adjusting it but couldn't seem to pull it off.

"Tell us what it's about."

Clink clink, knives and forks, a pulsing tension in the air.

"Well, I think it's about a guy who's losing his mind whilst trying to survive in the big city. But to be honest I haven't gotten that far yet" (chuckle) "so I'm not completely sure."

I'd been hoping for a sympathetic reciprocal chuckle and had received none. Greg had looked ready to offer one but a quick glimpse at the shrew and he'd reconsidered. Pussy-whipped houseboy that he was. The matriarch continued with her imperial glarings, staring daggers, spewing shards of ice into my face. I thought about how difficult it must be to live life like this, the sheer force it would require one to stay so permanently peeved. If you did it long enough I assumed you just dissolved into a pool of acid or something.

Once again, no response. She was showing me how stupid I was for not having an idea for the book yet, and how equally stupid I was for having been foolish enough to admit it in public. Eventually she started up with the small talk again, started telling me about some renovations they had planned for the house, this remodeling or that, but I wasn't really listening anymore because a panic of sorts had begun to seize me, something that was clawing at my throat and all but disallowing breath. This had happened to me a few times before, but not in a long while. The pressure rose up in my chest cavity, my heart started pumping way too hard and I was so dizzy I felt like I was going to pass out, just fall over out of the chair and die right there on their dining room carpet, the one they'd been telling me about, the one they'd had installed recently. Tara was still chattering away and Greg was chiming in on occasion and there I was, sitting there in mortal terror, unable to utter a single word, fighting for breath, on the edge of death. After a while they noticed.

"Jim, are you okay?" Greg asked.

He looked worried; Tara just looked annoyed. It wasn't proper behavior. Propriety again. Blast the world's propriety, I'm over here dying you know. Presently I was able to choke out a few words, by way of explanation.

"Yeah... I'm just not feeling too well," I said.

"Too much wine already?" Greg joked.

I grimaced a smile at him. "Excuse me," I said.

I got up, deposited the napkin in my seat and headed for the bathroom. Once there, I laved cold water on my face for a time and tried doing what I could to regroup. I couldn't face the idea of going back out there again. Maybe there was a back door I could use; yeah, I remembered, there was one in the kitchen, leading out onto the deck. Finally I gathered my strength and rejoined the fray.

"Listen, I'm really sorry but I think I have to go. I'm really not feeling well at all, not sure what happened. It just came over me like that."

"Very sorry to hear," said Tara. "Hope you feel better soon."

She didn't mean a word of it, she hoped it was something terminal. I don't think she even believed I was sick at all. I didn't care, all I wanted was to get out of there.

Greg walked me out. "Feel better man," he said giving me an encouraging pat on the back. I mumbled something further mid-stumble, waved in what I hoped was a socially acceptable farewell (or something approximating it), got in the car and drove off. The pain and dizziness and constriction in my chest all but vanished within a matter of minutes. It had been that shrew. I resolved then and there to avoid associating with women going forward, unless said association were absolutely life-threateningly unavoidable. They were all shrews, the lot of them. The man who invents asexual reproduction should be given a trillion dollars on the spot. Fine, I was a misogynist, but look at what they were doing to me, how else was I supposed to react. Even when they weren't spitting at you, they looked like they were preparing to; it was enough to stop your heart, enough to short out your brain. Why would God have created such a creature. Perhaps to test the will of men. But it was more than just women, if I was being totally honest with myself, that sort of thing was happening more and more often - not on quite the level it had occurred tonight, but the general trend was there. I was having more trouble functioning lately, increasing amounts of difficulty just going out in public. Give me a year and I was going to be just like Relative Ed. The world did this to you, this modern world of theirs with all its tricks and traps and everything all squeezed together like it was, everyone fighting to the death over scraps. I wanted to stop it, wanted to change direction and revert back to being the person I'd been when I was younger, but there didn't seem to be any way to do it, at least none that I could see. You could drink yourself into a stupor, drug yourself, I suppose. You could try to hypnotize yourself, the way I'd seen the others do, try to look the other way, tell yourself that everything was just fine, convince yourself that what you were seeing before your eyes every day wasn't there, but that only worked up to a point and then it stopped working altogether once you'd reached a certain age. The only solution was total abstinence, total withdrawal. It wasn't a solution I liked but there was no way around it. Stay in your house, or head for the hills. Find an unclaimed hiding spot, hunker down and stay there. Keep your head down and keep quiet. Stick to the shadows. Only go out at night, adapt, evolve, become nocturnal.

My thoughts were confused, I didn't really know what I wanted to do. I drove home, put the car down and went out for a walk to try to clear my head. It was getting late and no one else was around, I had the square all to myself. Morristown was dead, even more dead than usual. No cars were going by, even the wind had died down, you could hear a pin drop. The weather was actually nice, it was warm and balmy, unseasonably so, and yet the town always felt so cold and empty, no matter how many people they filled it up with. I guess most of the world was like that, if you stopped and thought about it. I walked in circles round the square like an old man, and all I could think of was how much I wanted to get out, just how badly I wished I was anywhere but there. There was no point to life if you were just going to go round in circles like this, circles of other peoples' devising, circles that made no sense, that didn't feel right, that never went anywhere except right back to where you'd started. They never gave you a second to breathe, didn't allow you a single solitary moment to think things over for yourself, you were so busy running around working and hustling and worrying about things that by the time you realized what was going on, it was too late, you were old, it was over, life had passed you by and you had nothing to show for it save thirty years' worth of paid bills. I'd read stories of others who'd gotten out, accounts of those who'd uncovered better alternatives, who'd gone out and seen the world, who'd fled and found whatever they'd fled to a vast improvement over the original scene. There was something behind the screen, something our masters didn't want us to see, some secret they had a vested interest in keeping preserved. I'd be damned if I lived out the rest of my life like this, like some bird in a cage, singing upon command. Tied to a dining room chair, talking about remodeling options, looking for my next fight just so that I could win it and go to bed feeling like a winner. I had to get out. I was ready for just about anything - I'd travel light, eat sandwiches, sleep on park benches, whatever it took. Risk the wrath of the propriety police, risk facing all that such carelessness entailed. Thumb my nose at the gods, see if there was a response. I sat down on a bench and stared up at the moon. All I could do was wish I was somewhere else.

14

So on top of all that, I was lonely. Damn lonely. I needed a girl, I was sick of being on my own. I'd been alone since college and it had just been way too long, it was time to find someone. Where, I had no idea. They were all hiding away in their houses or married or whatever, the whole situation was absurd. But I was determined to try. I'd thought about going back to the dommes but that whole thing was just as silly, even more so than the normal way, to be honest. Two hundred fifty dollars and all you got was a drained wallet and a bump on the head. Maybe a few bad tastes in your mouth to go along with it. It was basically a gyp. I supposed that it was the same for all the others though, too: you shot off and dropped your load and nothing really happened, nothing had changed, all you did was feel moderately better for about fifteen minutes or so and then you were right back to feeling like shit. It was silly being a man.

So in lieu of the dommes, I decided to go the conventional route, to try hitting up the bars. Morristown certainly had a lot of bars, I had to give it that; if you were thirsty you certainly could find a place to remedy the problem. They weren't places I wanted to go however. The clientele was decidedly discomfiting. Young upwardly mobile urban professionals, or whatever it was, that whole set, a bunch of twits bent on conquering the world; sneer a lot and get a raise. I'd long since given up on assimilation there. I was never going to get behind their little movement, the yuppies could do their thing and I'd do mine. But the bars were where the chicks were at so I had to go there.

I went there. It was a Friday night and the place was wall-to-wall humanity. The vibes were the same as ever, i.e. hostile as all hades. The hipsters, the in-crowd, the chic and self-involved. I fought the panic down and squeezed myself in at the bar to do some drinking, see if maybe that helped. Three beers later and miraculously it had, at least a little bit. I'd been apprehensive as results lately had been decidedly mixed - sometimes it helped and sometimes it hindered, and sometimes it just did nothing. That night things were working okay though. Two young chicks were sitting on my left. A few more tickings of the clock and then the one closest made the mistake of turning around.

"How ya doin'," I asked, smiling.

She scoffed. I hadn't quite pounced but I was doing it all wrong anyway, as always. Those long-lashed eyes went batting around, considered the wall, then came back to rest on me. She'd decided she was bored, why not. Nothing better to do.

"I'm doin' okay, how bout you."

"I'm doin' just fine. Wondering why there's never anything to do in the world."

Resumption of scoffing. "What are you *talking* about?" A serious deviation from the usual script. Lip curling, looking around for a weapon.

"I dunno, I'm just bored with things in general."

"And so you came to the bar to complain about it?"

"Not really."

"So why are you here?"

"Searching for signs of life, I suppose."

A short burst of derisive laughter, followed by a rapidly turned back. I figured that was it but then when I looked again the two of them were now facing me in tandem.

"This one says he's looking for signs of life," the original chick said to her friend, showing me off like I was some exhibit in a zoo. The two of them looked exactly the same, completely identical in every way, like clones of each other, each with the same look on their face, the same makeup, the same hairstyle, the same clothes, everything. The attention to detail was staggering. Even the voices were the same. There was a prototype and they'd multiplied it out about a billion times and now the world had been coated over in little chick drones, perfectly synchronized, all of them chattering and yammering away in unison, and every few seconds one of them got married and left the pool but there were always more waiting to take her place. It was like they turned them out of some chick factory. Probably somewhere in the Midwest. Perhaps there was a way of breaking into the factory and altering the formula. Fiddle with the sanity knob, change the setting to civil.

"So have ya found any yet?" the second one asked. Signs of life, she meant.

"No, I haven't."

"Well keep looking."

That was it, they turned back around. I'd been dismissed. "I will," I said under my breath.

Well, that had gone about as well as expected. That was basically what I'd remembered from before, from the last time I'd tried. I finished my beer and went back out on the green. I could breathe again. The stars were out and the evening air felt nice. What a fucking world.

15

I went to work for another few weeks with Christine driving me crazy and I was about to bust a nut. I thought about going into New York to pick up a hooker. I thought about going gay. I thought about a whole lot of things, none of them good. I thought about becoming homeless, about robbing a bank, about selling out and doing things their way. There were lots of options and yet there weren't any, not really. The world was a sinful, shameful place, asshole on top of asshole, joke upon joke, just one dead end after another, a colossal waste of time. It was seriously getting me down. I decided to get drunk, really drunk, I mean, like I used to in college. I sat in my room for about two hours and pounded the beers down one after another and then went out to stagger around on the street, just to see what would happen. Half my brain was telling me I was going to wind up getting arrested but I didn't really care. At least that's how the other half was responding. I lurched along the sidewalk, my eyes all wrong, peering into every nook and cranny, going everywhere at once. The girls were veering out of the way and the guys looked like they were going to hit me.

After one of them actually spun around and challenged me to a fight, I decided to get my drunk ass off the street and hide out for a few minutes. You tried to live a little and you wound up either in jail or in the hospital. With a throbbing headache the next morning either way.

I ducked into a diner and plopped myself down in a booth in the corner. There was no one else there, just me and the waitress and a cook in the back. The place was brilliantly white, it was hurting my eyes. The waitress came over to bring me a menu. She was plump and friendly-looking. I ordered a coffee. She brought it over. She saw I was drunk but realized that I was harmless and decided to stay for a chat.

"You're looking a little the worse for wear, aren't ya there sport?" she asked with a big cheerful condescending grin, resting one flabby forearm on the table.

"A little the worse for wear, you don't hear that expression all that often these days," I said. Or at least that's what I tried to say, it probably came out a little different. The ole lips weren't quite up to the task.

Her smile faded a little, the jovial tone changed somewhat. "You okay?" she asked. She was concerned. I mean, for real, she meant it, no bullshit or anything. I didn't answer, I just went quiet. I thought about asking her for her number but didn't do it. She really wasn't my type anyway. But she sure was nice. Every so often one of them was nice. It was like a miracle whenever you saw it.

Another customer came in, the waitress went for the menus and I was left to my own devices again. I drank my coffee down and went back outside. I was sick and tired of the green and so I angled down the street going the other way. I walked and walked, I went until I was well outside the town limits and then walked some more. There were no people around. The solitude was addicting. I was going to walk until the lights faded as well, until there was no sign of them anywhere to be seen, until the stench of it had been cleared from my nostrils. Eventually I sobered up and realized how tired I was, how far I'd gone. Goddamn if I wasn't halfway to

Hackettstown. I didn't recognize where I was, it was some sort of country road with the sidewalk gone and the wind blowing and all. You had to walk a good long way in Jersey to find this sort of thing. I began to worry I'd gone too far. There were no cars coming by and the temperature had dropped significantly and all I was wearing was a flimsy little short-sleeved shirt. Back in the day you could have thumbed a ride at this point but those days were long gone. Looked like I'd just have to suck it up and hump it back in. As I did so I reflected on what I'd just done. It made no sense sober, but then again few things did. I reflected on the utter foolishness of my life, the humiliating cringe-inducing turn of recent events, the injuries I'd been forced to bear, whether from external sources or self-inflicted. I was able to draw no conclusions from the data. Upon examining the facts of the case, I'd looked upon the verdict and found it lacking.

I went home and climbed into bed and slept for about twenty-four hours. I skipped work, I skipped meals, I skipped the whole damn thing. I was hungover for sure, but I was getting the feeling I would have stayed in bed either way, whether I'd been drunk the night before or not. The next stop was the loony bin. Once again I didn't care.

16

It was a few days later. Sitting there in my cube, things were getting to me. Even more than usual, I mean. One of the younger kids had stopped by to talk shop and it was all I could do not to slap him. Some of these guys ate, drank and slept this computer shit, it was unthinkable, it made me sick. Careers be damned. I was busy drowning in the depths of despair when suddenly Greg's face appeared in the doorway. He was smiling for no reason, at least none that I could see.

"Sorry about the other night," I said. I felt compelled to say something about it.

"No problem. How ya feeling?"

There was no way I was going to answer that question honestly. In fact, I figured I'd take it in the opposite direction, just for kicks, just to amuse myself. "As right as rain," I replied, offering up a smile even goofier than his.

"Stanley is going to show us that demo at two, he wants to meet over in conference room B," said Greg.

"There is nothing I would rather do," said I.

He was still smiling, those googly eyes googling. If he didn't stop smiling I was going to throw the keyboard at him. Attached to anything or not.

Around eleven, Christine came by for a word. I wasn't in the mood to be tormented and so I just tried not looking at her, tried shelving my naked lust for the time being. One of these days she was going to see what was hidden behind my eyes and call the cops on me or something. She was talking all technical and it was hurting my head, she'd said the name 'Richard' and turned a touch more red and then she'd said something that necessitated a response and the words 'I quit' had been right on the edge of my tongue but I hadn't said them, I refrained. I didn't know how much longer I could last, regardless of whether there were any options or not. I'd lost the thread of what Christine was saying and she was staring down at me, the optical equivalent of hands on hips.

"Jim - did you hear what I just said?" she asked.

"Indeed," I said. I hadn't heard a word. Mercifully she just gave up and went away. Guess it hadn't been all that important after all.

Greg and I went down to the cafeteria for lunch.

"Tara said she had a nice time the other night," Greg said.

"No she didn't," I said. It had just come out of my mouth, I'd thought it but hadn't intended to say it.

"What?" Greg said, all but dropping his sandwich. I was too tired to apologize or try to talk my way out of it.

"Never mind," I said. Greg glowered, I continued eating. It didn't matter. All was folly.

I was on the edge. I was losing control of myself. It was get out or die. I felt trapped, desperate, like a hunted animal backed into a corner. I was starting to feel like if they squeezed me just a little bit harder I was going to explode, as in literally, physically, explode in a shower of flesh and blood and guts with my organs and innermost parts flying all over the place, covering them all in one final protest, a most organic of objections – one last bloody cataclysmic fuck-you, one that would brook no response, would allow no gainsaying, would entertain no counteroffers, would leave no room for interpretation whatsoever. The ultimate final word, you might say.

So in the interest of avoiding spontaneous combustion and staving off utter disaster, I decided to take a week's vacation. I had some time coming to me so there was no problem. I sat around at home trying to decide where to go. There were lots of candidates but none that jumped right out at me, nothing that leapt up and grabbed me by the throat and said 'pick me, go here'. Finally I decided on Canada. I'd been to Toronto once but I'd never been to Quebec. Montreal, that was it - I'd heard good things about Montreal, I'd go up there and see what that place was all about. It was still too early in the season and it was going to be a bit too chilly, but screw it, I had to go somewhere. So Canada it was.

I threw a few things into a bag and headed out. Up the Thruway I went, through towns and cities, through great forests of pine. In a matter of hours I was at the border, handing my credentials over to a big burly fellow, a scowling guard who looked like he hadn't gotten laid in about a year. He let me through. I proceeded.

A few hours later I was in Montreal. The city was nice, in a grey, dreary sort of way. There was a big hill off to one side, Mount Royal or something. Montreal was known for its bar scene, there were supposed to be quite a few of them up there. I waited til nightfall and then went in search of them.

I found them. They were the same as the ones in Jersey. More hipster snobs, Jesus Christ, they were everywhere, even up there in Canada where the people were supposed to be so much nicer. The world had been overrun, it was besieged, it had been plowed under. I took as much of it as I could take, drank one more beer for good luck and returned streetside. It was bloody cold in Montreal, even the heavy jacket I'd brought along was proving inadequate. It had been drizzling off and on for hours and now it was turning to snow, a light flurry coming down and sprinkling the streets like it was Christmas in April. I passed a strip club and went inside. Montreal was also known for its strip clubs; it was a tourist attraction of sorts, or so I'd heard. I went up the steep flight of stairs, sat myself against the wall and let the girl bring me a drink. She was overweight and all dressed up like some sort of clown, and she was speaking with this outrageous French accent that I suddenly found rather humorous. When she caught me smirking, she objected, then after a few sharp words of revenge she stormed off. The only word of French I knew was 'merde' and I'd only heard it thrown in about four or five times in one sentence. So I'd laughed, so what, so shoot me. What could you do, you were prisoner to your moods. A slave to circumstance, a marionette dancing to mischievous tunes, yanked about on the most capricious of strings. I'd been writing too much lately, my thoughts were starting to sound literary.

So the first whore had shoved off and the others had seen what had happened and were leaving me well alone and so I sat there and drank and watched the show instead. Bright lights and flashes of flesh, a bunch of drooling greaseballs, a seriously dismal scene, real dregs of humanity shit. These places never made much sense to me, I mean what could really happen. No one was going home with anybody and all you did was run the risk of blowing a whole lot of cash. I drank myself into a stupor nonetheless and stumbled back out into the snow at god only knew what hour. It was late on a Saturday night, well past conventional closing time and yet the sounds of revelry still lingered; the city definitely liked to party. And as usual, I couldn't find a way to plug myself into any of it. I was the world's original lonely man, a pariah, destined to wander the face of the earth forever alone. Most nights when I got that drunk, it didn't really bother me anymore. I suppose that was the whole point of the exercise. I lumbered back to the hotel and passed out face-first on the bed. Mission accomplished.

The next morning I decided I'd had enough of Montreal already and so I continued on my way. I had the whole week to myself and didn't feel like going back home yet, especially without anything having happened yet. Quebec City was supposed to be somewhere just down the road, I'd go check that out. I'd never really heard anything about Quebec City, had never heard anyone talk about it or knew anyone who'd been there and so I knew next to nothing about the place. Oh well, it was there, and it was only a few hours away.

I got there just before dark, put the car down and went looking for a place to eat. There was a quaint little restaurant on the outskirts of town, like a little doll house with its white doilies on the table and lace curtains on the windows and all. It didn't look like my kind of place but I went in anyway, I was hungry. Everyone inside was speaking French and were looking at me strangely, they didn't want me in there. It had been a bad idea to go in but now for good old propriety's sake I couldn't very well just turn around and leave, so I got myself a little table for one, sat down and stared out the window and just waited it out. I had some kind of chicken dish that was pretty good, but the waitress was being so unfriendly I couldn't really enjoy it too much.

When I walked back outside, I realized how tired I was. And more than a little hungover. I wasn't ready for the city yet, all I wanted to do now was crash. I went back to a seedy motel I'd passed on the way in, got myself a room there and then went next door to the roadhouse bar for a quick nightcap. Once again, a real locals place, all French, a floating sea of distrustful eyes trying to stare me into the ground. I was tired and I'd had enough, I ignored them, I went up to the bar and got a Labatts and started drinking it down. There was a hockey game on TV, the Canadiens were playing. Next to me was a huge oaf in a flannel shirt, with greasy grey hair and heavily weathered skin. He looked like a lumberjack or something. He probably was. He was ignoring me and I was ignoring him back. Fuck this French shit, I was going to drink my beer whether they liked it or not. The Canadiens scored a goal, a heavy-duty slapshot from way outside. "Nice shot," I said, more to myself than anyone else. The lumberjack looked over at me.

"Yoo like 'okee?" he asked.

I told him I did. His entire demeanor changed, in an instant, the guarded veneer melted away within seconds and now he was smiling and talking and ordering shots of whiskey and everything. Within about twenty minutes we were the best of friends, bosom buddies, almost like family, drinking our shots down and babbling on and slapping each other on the back. We talked hockey for the most part, that was our common ground. My new brother's name was Yves, he told me he'd played in the minor leagues once, way back in the day, had even played with Guy Lafleur (which if you knew anything about hockey was a pretty big deal). I wasn't sure if I believed him or not but he was certainly big enough, he looked the part. Maybe he'd been an enforcer, a goon, a third or fourth line guy.

Yves and I drank together for the rest of the night and closed the place down. The rest of the locals saw the reaction I'd gotten from one of their own and they'd warmed up to me, not in terms of direct interaction but more by way of a warm wafting vibe; I'd been accepted, I was in the club and would be allowed to stay there, at least for the night. The humans were a downright suspicious lot but their company could be quite reassuring once you'd broken down the barriers and put yourself on the right side of them.

Yves stumbled off and I stumbled off and I located my motel room and once again fell face-first on the bed and passed out. I often wondered if I was an alcoholic. Probably not yet, but I had potential. Another few years and I'd be part of that club too. The things we had to look forward to.

The morning dawned bright and early, and damn cold. These Canadian Springs were not for me, the cold just got into your bones and camped out there, refusing to budge. Next time I was going south. Charleston or something, maybe Savannah. My energy level was low but I was determined to see something of the city, I hadn't gone all that way for nothing. Quebec City felt a bit like Europe, or at least as much like Europe as I imagined it might. I'd never been to Europe so it was pretty much a guess. Although I had seen a few English shows on TV. As in English, from England, taking place in England. Not in terms of the language being spoken. But anyway, Quebec City was probably closer to France than England, the tone of the place for sure. Parts of it were almost medieval, with the towers and turrets and old stone walls and things. I wound my way up to a wide open terrace and had a look round; the view was nice, stupendous even. To the north was the rest of the Great White North. It looked brown. They should have called it the Great Brown North. I stood there in the breeze and watched all the people, the couples strolling hand in hand, the families milling around. The French and all these people in another country, all worlds apart, complete mysteries, all unknowable and destined to remain that way. Whole lives I'd never know anything about. Lives better than my own. I didn't have a life, I hadn't been able to acquire one for myself yet. I didn't know how you did it. I'd done the same things they'd all done, for the most part, grown up, gone to school, got out, gotten a job, and yet all I had to show for it was a pair of boxes to alternate between. The cube and the apartment, one duller than the next. I didn't want to go back, and yet what else was there to do. What was I going to do, keep going north? Become an eskimo? I supposed I could try but I doubted it would go very well, as I'd never been terribly self-sufficient. I'd never make it as a survivalist. I didn't even know how to fish. I could barely make it as an apartment-dweller, if I was being completely honest. I lived by the grace of the surrounding system. I guess you could say I liked to bite the hand that fed me. It was an abusive hand though, so I didn't really feel all that guilty about doing it.

I wandered around Quebec City for another few days, had another few meals, listened to some more French and then when I'd had enough I got back into the car and headed home. I'd hoped the trip would reenergize me but all I felt was tired. As you got older, whenever your battery drained down like that it became harder and harder to recharge it; it was like you had a finite amount of juice to spend before the thing was dead and then that was it, you were through, you didn't want to move anymore, didn't want to do anything at all. Mentally I was prepared to 'rage against the dying of the light', but physically I felt otherwise. Like they said, the old spirit was willing but the flesh was weak. I was getting old already.

17

No sooner did I get home when I was served with a parental warrant demanding my presence at dinner. All these people ever wanted to do was go out for dinner. The thought of it made me choke. This wasn't just dinner, it was dinner out, at one of my Dad's fancy-ass restaurants, the places he liked to take his clients to show them how fucking important he was. The restaurant was this chic expensive place we'd gone to about a million times before, with everything all done up real special, with all the waiters and waitresses falling all over you in the hopes they'd get a few gold coins tossed their way at the end, you know, alms to the poor and all that. We sauntered in like conquering heroes and sat down at the table. We were surrounded by rich pricks, they were all around us, on every side. Everywhere you looked there was another rich prick, either smirking or frowning. I wanted to retch. The waiter came with the menus, we ordered. I had no appetite but I ordered something anyway. Two bottles of wine came out, corks were popped and glasses were filled. The opening ceremony was over, the preliminaries complete. On to the next round. So far the score was even.

"Jake's not doing so well," my mother said. "You should go and see him. He's your brother, you know."

Jake was never doing well so that wasn't exactly news. I didn't go there though. I told her I'd go and see him soon. Even though I knew full well he had no interest in seeing me.

"So how's the job going?" Dad asked. The money, always the money.

"It's not going so well, actually, if you want me to be honest about it. I'm thinking about quitting."

I was supposed to have said 'fine' but I wasn't in the mood for games; if he wanted to ask a question I was going to give him an answer.

"Jim..." It was a growl, like a dog warning me off.

"Here we go again," my mother said.

"Don't do anything you'll regret later on," my father said.

It was like a broken record, I'd heard it all before. I could predict the replies before they were made. I started chewing on the fork to keep myself from yelling. We finished the first bottle of wine and started on a second. The dinner came. I'm sure it tasted good but I didn't want to eat any of it and so it just sat there in front of me. I looked at the food, watched my parents eating. There was something unbelievably disturbing about the whole thing.

"Why aren't you eating anything?" my mother asked.

"Because I'm not hungry."

"We take you to this nice restaurant and you don't eat anything. Real nice."

I looked at my father, sitting there in his fancy suit and tie, all smug and satiated and self-assured, like he was one of the illuminati or something. He was an arrogant blowhard, a wolf in wolf's clothing, a bourgeois pig. The sight of him induced nausea. Suit man, golf man, know-it-all man, cigar-chompin' scotch-drinkin' stock market man, the be-all end-all of the whole fucking universe. Jake and I were apples far from the tree and I couldn't have been happier about it if you'd shot me up with morphine. Look at him as he sits there sipping his after-dinner liqueur, his amaretto or whatever the hell it was, sitting there without a care in the world, bushy little mustache going up and down, beady little eyes going back and forth. It was all just for him, wasn't it.

"So are you going to call Jake?" my mother asked. "He's really down, you know, he could use your help."

"What's wrong with him?" I asked.

Granted, a smartass thing to say. Maybe I just wanted to get under her skin a little.

"Oh, Jim... You know the story. He's depressed, he's not feeling well. He never goes out anymore, doesn't do anything, he never talks to anyone."

"He needs to get a better job," said Dad.

"And he's always talking about moving out on his own – which I think would be good for him – but the problem is he doesn't have any money to do it with," Mom continued. "So I agree with your father, a proper career of some sort might help."

"Jake couldn't survive on his own. He'd starve to death."

They didn't like the response but instead of complaining about it they opted for silence. I didn't feel like talking anymore and they could see it, which of course was why my mother had to bring it up again about a minute later. She was like a pit bull, she could never let things drop.

"So you'll call your brother?" she asked.

"Yes, I'll call him," I said.

Jesus Christ. I'll call anybody if you'll just stop talking. The check came, my Dad paid it. We collected ourselves and went outside to wait for the valet to retrieve the Lincoln. My Dad gave the kid a few bucks, the kid said 'thank you sir.' We got in the car and left. My parents were in good spirits on the way home, it appeared they had enjoyed themselves. The world was still operating according to their design.

I sat in bed that night and stared at the ceiling. Restaurants and road trips, this was supposed to be enough, this was the fuel to go on. You had to be lobotomized to fall for it. A hundred hours of drudgery and they gave you one at the end to stuff your face with and everyone called it even. For the life of me I couldn't understand why more people didn't go crazy, didn't go stark raving mad and start running around in the streets yelling about it. We'd been bamboozled, we'd been scammed, fooled, cheated, lied to at every turn. Where was the outrage, where was the response? Humanity had been asleep from the beginning. It was a race full of sheep who didn't mind following each other around all day long, who didn't mind being tortured to death as long as the right people were telling them it was necessary. My Dad sat there in his fancy restaurant eating his fancy dinner and he'd only had to give up every single hour of every single day of his entire godforsaken life to earn the honor; that thought never even crossed his mind. I mean what the hell was wrong with him, what was wrong with people in general. And there I lay with all my supposedly enlightened thoughts and ideas and I couldn't think of a way out either. What the hell was wrong with me too.

18

Another dream about Tracey. A collage of snapshots, shifting and blending, a moving kaleidoscope. First she's sitting on the bed in my dorm room, laughing, lips parted, eyes half closed, head tilted back, like a movie star all sultry and seductive, like Marilyn Monroe, but it's not for me yet, she's waiting to be kissed by Martin, this is before, when he still had her, and their faces are just inches apart and he's about to do it and I'm so jealous I could throw something at them. Then the scene changes and we're out in front of the apartment complex having a snowball fight and it's January and frigid cold and I'm wearing my blue and white sweater the one I hoped Tracey would like and we're running between the cars dodging and trying to pelt each other with snowballs and Tracey is laughing and everything is free and easy for a change, and then we go back inside where it's warmer and she cuddles up next to me on the couch and lets me wrap my arms around her, and it's nice, so nice, she's mine now, she's with me, not with that other jerk, the one who'd treated her so badly for so long. Now I could treat her right, could show her how much better things could be, could shelter her, protect her, make her love me the way I loved her, the way I always had. And then we're in Rochester, sitting on a different couch, we're at her parents' house and it's six months later and she hasn't let me kiss her in so long and it's making me sick and I take her chin with my finger trying to tilt it towards me and she resists, she hardens, goes rigid, and it fills me with pain and so I try again, I try to kiss her and she pulls away, like I'm garbage, filth, meat that's gone off, like I don't exist, like I'm absolutely nothing. She's back to watching her movie again acting like nothing has happened but what has actually happened is that it's all over, it's ended, the dream has died and there'll be no more. That scene washes away and now I'm sitting in a bar and Tracey is the bartender, she's wearing a baggy grey sweatshirt and her hair is all tousled and piled up on top of her head, and she won't come down to give me a drink, she's just standing there at the other end, staring me down with her steely grey eyes. I try walking over to her end to see if it improves things any but now the bar has suddenly filled up and I can't get through, there are too many people and they're all crowding together and pushing and shoving and jostling me around, and I can't get to her, no matter what I do, I can't get the drink. The lights go out and all is black and then they come on again and I'm back out in the snow, cold and listless, watching the cars go by. Waiting for Spring.

19

Will was in town, he was visiting me this time. We were going into the city so that he could play an open mic. Open mic was when the amateurs all got up to play for nothing. I'd watched him do it a few times before. Most of the time it was pretty horrible, but every so often someone got up there who could really play, who turned your head around and made you listen.

We talked on the train. "So how are things?" I asked.

"I'm putting out an album," Will said.

My heart stopped. "You mean you got signed?"

"Naw, just doing it on my own."

My heart started again. Good.

"How's your writing going?" he asked.

"Shitty for the most part. Although I did a short story the other night that came out okay. It was about college, actually."

Will didn't say anything else. He knew better than to bring Tracey up. He was probably just assuming the story was about her, although it hadn't been.

The train pulled into Penn Station and we got off. "Do you know where we're going?" I asked.

"Sort of," Will said.

That meant no. He told me where it was (a bar over in the Village), I helped him sort out the subway lines and in short order we were there. It was a tiny little railroad car of a place, fairly crowded, with as much crap in it as people, knickknacks and trinkets all over everything, debris really. The place looked like a pawn shop more than a bar. Little gnomes and trolls, strange antique lamps, handcrafted carvings from somewhere down in the third world. There was a giant mannequin standing over the bar, right up against the mirror, a hot chick with big tits and long legs and gauze for clothes. No less plastic than the others, if you asked me.

We got beers and turned to face the stage, a miniscule space under bright lights way back in the caboose. A girl with long stringy hair was up there crooning; she didn't look at all nervous, she looked quite pleased with herself really and her friends sitting there at the tables looked equally pleased. This in spite of the fact that the music she was playing was so bland it could have passed for ambient noise. Truth be told, I didn't really like going to these things at all, I found them tedious as hell but Will kept dragging me along and so I went. Watching this girl preen, I tried to understand what made her feel so enthusiastic about what she was doing. The music was no good and there were only about four people back there watching her play, it all seemed rather silly to me. The rush of performing and all that. I'd never have made it as a musician, I didn't have a musician's soul. I had to hide away in my hole all solitary-like to get anything done.

The girl finished up and then the next guy got up to play. I was already on my third beer. If you drank enough beer you didn't mind it too much. This guy was tall and lean and was wearing a black body-length trench coat, looking all sinister and grim, like a musical gangster or something. He didn't have a guitar or anything, it was just him and his body-length trench coat. He pulled a harmonica out of his pocket. Without a word to the crowd, he started puffing into it. Hard. Then he started screaming. It was singing I supposed but it was loud as hell and it was really angry. The bar had taken notice of this guy, he'd managed to get everyone's attention, which I knew from past experience was hard to do at one of these open mic things. He was vigorously singing and huffing and puffing away and doing a fair bit of gyrating and gesticulating while he did it, and then the next thing we knew he was throwing himself down on the floor and convulsing like an epileptic having a fit, flopping around on his back like a dying fish fighting for air. I'd never seen anything like it. The rest of the world hadn't either, it was the first time it had ever been done. He was flopping and wheezing and flailing around on the floor and still playing the harmonica the whole time, it was like some kind of magic act, I didn't see how he was doing it. When he got back up again his face was beet red and he was breathing extremely heavily into the microphone, the performance looked like it had just about finished him off. Finally he stopped. His trenchcoat had ripped a little on one side and I thought I could see some blood trickling down from somewhere near his hairline, or maybe it was just bruised. Chest heaving, heavy panting, breath going in and out, his hair all in his face and covering his eyes and everything. He was utterly spent. It had either been an epiphany of sorts or a complete mental breakdown. The crowd gave him a round of applause, more than they'd given the first girl but still nothing to write home about. Another reason to dislike open mics - this guy had just about lost his life in pursuit of a great performance and the goddamn nitwits had barely even noticed. Well, they'd noticed but hadn't really acknowledged it. You know what I mean.

"Can you top that?" I asked Will, leaning in closer so he could hear.

"Will have to try," he said.

It was his turn next. He got his guitar out of the case and shuffled over to the stage. He went up there and did his set and it was the same thing, no one even noticed. The sound was so low you almost couldn't hear him play. I felt sorry for him, his songs were really good and this was the only place he ever got to play them and no one could even hear it and no one really cared. More futility. Futility everywhere. I was tired of futility, I wanted to spit in its eye, jump up and down on top of it and trample it into the dust. Every so often something was supposed to go right, or at least improve a little, and yet it never did. We were all stuck on a continual downward slide with no chance of arresting our descent, we were in a constant state of freefall, the whole thing was just sickening. Will was never going to get his music heard, I was never going to get my book published. No one was ever going to get laid again. It was pointless, we might as well just die and get it over with. Greg had called me a pessimist the other day. I got what he was saying, but by the same token I'd always just considered pessimists to be people who were paying more attention than the rest. Bad things kept happening to you and so you started expecting bad things to happen, it only stood to reason.

Anyway, Will wrapped up his set, the crowd did their obligatory little hand-clapping routine and Will and I went back to drinking. I kept looking over at him, searching for signs of the same sort of satisfaction that had appeared to consume the first girl, the one who'd gone up there earlier in the night, but I couldn't really tell either way; he remained veiled in neutrality, his expression as impassive as ever. Like I said, Will had always been a hard book to read. He played things close to the vest.

We hit a few more bars in the Village that night and then (somehow) wound up in the Bowery. Will had tracked down another place with live music. He was attracted to these places like a moth drawn to a flame, he had a preternatural ability to sniff them out from miles away. This bar was really hopping, a young and raucous crowd, lots of chicks around shaking their asses and letting their hair hang down. They felt safe in packs. It was making me want to drink more, and so I drank more. The other guys around me were hitting on them, finding success, going off into dark corners to do a little hobnobbing, a little smooching, a little prelude to the old horizontal mambo. Will and I sat there rather morosely and imbibed.

"How's Priti?" I asked him.

"She's good, things are going pretty well."

"You get laid yet?"

"Yeah, a lot. This girl is into it, believe it or not, you can't tell by looking at her but she's at least half a nympho."

Thoughts flashed of the night we'd had a month earlier, the blowjob that never was. I looked around the room with dull deadened eyes. I was getting gloomy and there was nothing I could do about it. I hated when I got this way. It happened a lot, to be honest. Will saw what was happening and stepped in to intervene, he knew my moods at this point better than I did.

"Shots," he said.

"Shit," I said.

I'd had too much already. But the shots came anyway and there was no choice but to dispose of them properly. Now I was really drunk. I was fucked up, if I'm allowed to use the more casual terminology. Manhattan was now veering left and right or maybe it was me and before long I was jumping up and smacking the metal signs just to hear them go bang and Will was drunk too and was howling at the moon or perhaps at the passing chickery I couldn't be sure which and by the time we got back to the train we were both about ready to puke. I have no idea how we were allowed to board the train. I had a way of pulling things together at the last minute when absolutely necessary, such as when going to ticket counters to purchase tickets and things like that and this had probably been one of those times, although I had no real memory of the event. The train rumbled along. Will passed out with his head resting against the window and I dozed a bit myself and it was exceedingly difficult getting back off again at the other end but we managed it all right. Apparently. I woke up the next morning in my own bed so I couldn't see any other possible explanation.

20

I'd called Jake up and he'd agreed to come over. We were sitting at the kitchen table, playing chess and drinking beer. Jake didn't really drink much beer and I was kind of surprised he'd accepted when I'd offered him one. We hadn't talked much yet but he seemed okay to me, didn't seem any worse than he'd ever been before. Then again, who really knew.

I took a sip of beer and jumped in. "Mom says you're not feeling so good."

"Don't listen to Mom."

"What is it, just the same old stuff?"

"There's nothing wrong." He moved his queen. Jake was a smart kid, he was better than me at chess but so far I was holding my own.

"You need to get outta that supermarket, that's half the problem right there."

"Don't start with the Dad shit."

"Fine, don't tell me anything. See if I care."

Jake got up and went to the fridge, came back with another bottle of beer. He sat down and made another move.

He was doing well as usual, I was just about screwed already and we'd only been playing about ten minutes. My mind was only half on the game however, the other half was on how I could get him to open up. The more I looked at him the more I saw that things definitely weren't quite kosher, his hands were shaky and his eyes were doing a little twitching. He'd had some of that in the past but it had gone away, and here it was, back again.

"I hear you're thinking about moving out."

"Of course."

"Where ya gonna go?"

"Anywhere. Away from here. Into the wilderness."

"The wilderness?"

"Yeah. Just wander off into the wilderness, never be seen again. Go off to Colorado or something, head into the mountains."

I looked at him to see if he was kidding and honestly it didn't look like he was.

"You serious?"

"What if I am?"

We dropped it for a while. Jake beat me within the next five minutes and we went into the other room to sit and watch some TV. There was nothing on so I just picked a movie at random and we pretended to watch it.

"Mom's worried about you, you know."

"What do you want from me, she worries."

"Come on, Jake. Why don't you tell me what's going on."

He blew up. "Look, why is everyone so worried about me all of a sudden?? Nobody ever gave a shit before. Everyone's acting like I'm doing something wrong, I'm not doing anything. I wish you'd all just get off my fucking back." He leapt from the couch and stormed off, slamming the door behind him. And that was that.

I sat there thinking about it some more. Jake was clearly on the edge, but the question was how much. I mean, I was on the edge myself so I could certainly relate, but being on the edge and going over the side were two entirely different things.

To an extent I agreed with my mother; Jake wasn't all right, there were some real signs of instability there. He was a volcano ready to blow, for sure. But so was I. Who was I to give him any advice. I mean, you said the right things, said a few words of encouragement, did your duty to god and country and then you let the cards fall where they may, right? Right? Was that it? Was I supposed to be doing more? And what could be done, really? The world was a shit place, I mean most of us knew it, we just had differing amounts of trouble dealing with it. Okay, someone couldn't cope, someone went off the deep end, and you gave that person meds or put them in a nice safe secure place and you hoped that made some sort of difference. But the other way of looking at it was that this was my brother, my own flesh and blood. He was someone I knew well, who I'd grown up with, someone who I was supposed to be helping out when he was in trouble. The long and short of it was that I didn't really know what to do for him. He was pissed at the world and I didn't really blame him and that was probably where it would have to be left. If my mother wanted to call in the cavalry, she could. Good luck with that though - Jake was a stubborn bastard, they were liable to get nowhere fast. And yet my brother's plight stayed with me that night, through another few beers, through a walk around town, through another night of laying in bed getting no sleep at all. I imagined what it was like for him, trapped within his own mind, injured, alone, unsure of where to turn for help. He was in a bad spot. And there was something different there now, something I couldn't quite put my finger on, a look in his eye that had never been there before. Or maybe it was all just my imagination. What the hell did I know anyway.

21

Sitting at the desk, pounding my brains out. Ten o' clock at night. Not the slightest shred of inspiration, not the tiniest little spark of light, nothing, nothing at all. About ready to die. My palms are actually sweating I'm so worked up about it. Frustration so thick you could cut it with a knife, so maddening I'm about to bash my head against the desk. The room is closing in. The air is too heavy, it doesn't feel right, makes my breathing feel too labored. I'm supposed to be a writer, I can feel it somewhere inside, hear it rattling around in there making all sorts of noise, and yet it just won't work, the words won't come. What must be done to draw yourself out of yourself. I drop my forehead down between my folded arms and smack it against the edge of the desk, lightly at first, then harder, in the hopes it might jog something loose. It doesn't help, nothing comes out.

I've been sending out the stuff I have somehow managed to write and the results have not been good. One rejection note after another, form letters telling me nothing whatsoever about all the things I'm presumably doing wrong.

The exercise is entirely pointless and yet I persist, week after week I send the shit out and the rejection notes come right back. I seriously must be mad. Talk about insanity being the act of doing the same thing over and over again and always expecting a different result, well, I'm the poster child for it. I've been beating my head against this wall for so long I've worn it right down to the skull. You can see the flesh clinging to the brick.

There's a bright spot though. Earlier in the week I'd sent out that story I'd written about college and had gotten a response back almost immediately; they said they liked it and wanted to include it in the next issue. It was just a rinky-dink little magazine, some fly-by-night thing no one had ever heard of with a circulation of about five, ten at most, but they said they were going to pay me thirty dollars for it so that made me feel pretty good. 'You're exactly what we've been looking for', the guy had said. He said it was the new style of writing, the modern style. I wasn't exactly sure what he meant by that but I was certainly happy to hear they'd liked it. Ecstatic even, if I'm being totally honest. For every hundred assholes who disapproved of your very existence, there was one who was prepared to accept it. The odds weren't good but I supposed it would have to do. What choice did I have. What choice did any of us have. We were all stuck on the same treadmill, being processed the same way. Swimming in the same insane waters. Lost in the apparatus, trapped in the innards of this great colossus, all iron and granite, some mindless devilry blown beyond all hope or scale, beyond the comprehension of man and god alike, a sleepless beast feasting on our spiritual marrow, oiled with lifeblood and greased with dreams, a churning burning hunk of machinery swallowing us up and spitting us out on a daily basis, forever primed and ready for more. There was no escape, but there was still hope for some relief. There, maybe I could put that in a book somewhere.

22

So I went back out to the bars and tried to pick up a girl. It was tough sledding for a few nights, no luck at all, and then on the third night I tried it I had some success. I was sitting in a place just off the green, a casual neighborhood spot, it was Thursday night around seven o'clock and the crowd was down. I'd just finished off a shepherd's pie and was staring at the wall. A girl came over for a chat, she said her name was Lily. She was dressed all in bright garish colors and had her hair cut way too short, it was all but chopped off; she looked like one of those weirdo chicks who deliberately does things all ass-backwards just to prove how interesting she was. I wasn't really in the mood for it but as we talked I realized she was actually kind of interesting and so I kept at it and soon we were going home together, going back to her place.

"I don't normally sleep with guys on the first date, but you're just so cool..." she oozed, laughing as we went through the doorway all tangled up together. I hadn't done anything that could be considered terribly cool, at least by my own estimation, I was just sort of assuming that she didn't get a whole lot of attention in general and was saying things off the top of her head just for the hell of it, just to have something to say. She really wasn't so good socially, to tell you the truth. The two of us were mildly drunk but no big deal really, nothing that would prove troublesome or throw up any roadblocks. Lily yanked her clothes off and lay down on her back.

"Come on over here, big boy..." she said.

Her arms were thrown back over her head and her eyes were half-closed. She had nice breasts. I stood there a moment longer, hesitating a bit. I wasn't normally too good with sex without certain other offbeat elements being introduced but I didn't really feel like having to explain anything to anyone and so I just dove right in, prepared to wing it and hope for the best. Things went pretty well and when we were finished Lily lit up a cigarette. It was the first time I'd noticed that the whole room smelled like an ashtray.

"Wow, that was good..." Lily said, blowing a thin stream of smoke into the air. "Was it good for you too, baby?"

"Yeah," I said.

I never liked it when chicks called you baby that quick, right off the bat like that. It was a little too clingy.

"How good?" she asked. Snuggling up next to me now.

"Real good," I said.

She was weird but she was cute. She had a spaced-out thing going on, the same as Will, but faster and more dazzled by things. There was something about her though, something in the way she talked, the way her eyes moved all funny, something suggestive of the fact that she wasn't all there. I began to suspect there were a few skeletons in the closet. Maybe a whole wardrobe full of them. This was the kind of chick who'd tell you she loved you, roll over and go to sleep, have a bad dream and wake up and stab you in the chest with a knife. Or maybe I was wrong, maybe she was just fine. I wasn't sure I was prepared to take the chance though. I lived a good deal of my life just operating on gut instinct and nothing else; so far it had gone pretty well.

I stayed about a half hour longer and then started getting my clothes back on.

"Am I going to see you again?" Lily asked.

"Yeah," I said.

She brightened up and gave me a peck on the cheek. She was wired, she had way too much energy for two o'clock in the morning, she was just chirping away the whole time I was pulling up my pants and then all the way out the door. As I walked down the steps I could still hear her inside, making all kinds of noise; now she was singing. Yeah, I was going to give this one a miss. i didn't like being lonely, sure, but companionship was occasionally life-threatening and I still wanted to live a little longer.

23

I rode along on a little wave of encouragement for awhile, swimming in the tides, buoyed by my recent success. It lasted about a week. I didn't call Lily and she didn't come looking for me with the knife. Life resumed normalcy. A few weeks went by and then I got a call from my mother. She told me that Jake had thrown some sort of fit and had broken a window. I told her I'd be over the following night.

The following night I went over. Jake was in his room, refusing to talk to anyone. I dragged him out and we went to the bar. We sat down on the stools and ordered beers. I waited for him to talk but as usual nothing was forthcoming. I was getting tired of trying to drag everything out of him.

"Mom said you broke a window," I said.

"Yeah," Jake said. He was avoiding eye contact.

"Why'd ya do that?"

"I was upset."

"About what?"

No answer. We drank our beers and ordered another pair. I looked at the ceiling, looked at the walls. I was getting tired of sitting around in bars but it was for a good cause this time and so I stuck it out. I was rewarded a few minutes later; Jake spoke.

"There's just no point in doing anything."

I looked over and saw there were tears in his eyes. It shocked me into total sobriety, I'd never seen my brother cry before, at least not since we'd been little kids. I started to reach for him, to give him a pat on the shoulder or something but then drew back, unsure of whether to do it or not.

"I know what you mean," I mumbled under my breath. I didn't really want him to hear it but couldn't help saying it either.

We both took slugs of beer. There were no more words after that, we just drank like that, side by side in perfect silence. I hoped that maybe just my presence alone might be soothing for him. I wanted to do something for him but felt somehow helpless, like nothing I said or did was going to make any difference at all. I didn't want to admit how much I understood what he meant, how much I felt like he did, how similar his thoughts were to mine. I was the wrong person to be trying to help him, I had real problems of my own, and yet there appeared to be no one else around to do it so I figured there was an obligation of sorts there. But nothing further was said, I couldn't find the words. We finished our beers and then I drove Jake home and went home myself. Once there, I couldn't sleep. There was a hole in my brother's heart and it needed filling. I was thoroughly disappointed in myself for not being able to offer more, for not being more helpful, more supportive. I hated the fact that Jake was being left there to try to sort everything out on his own. My parents were useless, my father was a plank of wood and my mother was liable to just throw drugs at him or something. But I didn't feel capable of helping him. I didn't feel capable of helping myself. Like the song said, we were islands to each other, and sometimes your own island became so intolerable that you reached across or got in a canoe and tried paddling but it was so damn difficult to find your way. I wasn't prepared to throw up my hands with Jake though, I was going to figure out a way to give him a hand. I didn't know what yet but I was going to figure something out, if it was the last thing I did.

24

But my own problems got in the way first. As the months passed and autumn became winter I sank into my own funk, slipped into my own hole, went all the way down to the bottom and just stayed there, refusing to budge. The days were dark and short. Work was horrible, I couldn't stand it anymore. I was beginning to change and I could feel it. My hair was getting longer and my patience was growing shorter, I felt incapable of even responding to half the shit people were saying to me. Greg sensed it and was beginning to shy away. For whatever reason Christine was now all but ignoring me, she was barely acknowledging my existence. I hadn't been given any new work to do in quite a long time and I was starting to wonder if they weren't about to fire me or something. Good, put me out of my misery. Do for me what I can't do for myself. I looked around the office and despaired. There the Bobbsey twins were, Clark and what's-his-name, that young pair of kids so bright-eyed and bushy-tailed and gung-ho about slaving away to the very best of their ability. There was Relative Ed, sitting in his little cave with his little goddamn plant, just the same as ever, typing away on his keyboard with ears smoking and brain circuits shorting. There I was, in the same exact place every single day of my fucking life. What a disaster. Life was simply too short for this.

I took some time off from work and stayed drunk for a week straight. Nothing changed, all that happened was I caught a cold. I sneezed and sniffled my way through February and onwards into March. I considered suicide. I went to the bars a few times and had arguments with a few people. Fuck me if the world wasn't leaning on me heavier than it had ever done before. I stopped calling my parents, stopped leaving the apartment, stopped eating meals, skipped lunch, skipped dinner, skipped the whole damn thing. There had to be change or things were going to end badly.

And then there was. Change arrived in the form of a revelation, a huge life decision made. I would go to California. I would go to California and sit in the sun and stay there until I'd rediscovered how to enjoy life, the way I'd done back when I was a kid. If the east coast was so intent on killing me then I would flee, I'd get the fuck out and go over to the west coast and see if that one treated me any better. Something told me it would. The weather alone would help, all that bright beautiful sunshine pouring down on you every day. It certainly couldn't hurt. All the oranges and palm trees and things, all that big blue pacific ocean. I went into Christine's office and put in my notice, she was surprised but didn't appear disappointed. I took one last longing look at those pretty shoes of hers, the ones I'd never been able to shine, and then went back out into the cube farm to await the moment of my release. Two weeks later it arrived. Free at last, free at last, thank god almighty I'm free at last.

25

The trip out didn't take too long, I drove like mad and made it in about three days. I'd thrown all my stuff in the car, as much as would fit, and I'd just gone. I'd barely told anyone I was leaving, I didn't want to be bothered. I'd told my parents obviously, and I'd told Will. I'd kind of mentioned it to Greg but almost in passing, he could piss off as far as I was concerned. Him and that wife of his. Just like all the rest. I was going to miss Will for sure, and I was worried about how Jake was going to make out, but as for everyone else I just didn't really care. I needed a break from them all. I needed a new start, and I needed it badly.

I grabbed a newspaper and took it to a seedy motel and went through the listings and within twenty-four hours had scored myself a room about four blocks from the beach. Things were brutally expensive in San Diego and pickings were slim, people were telling me later on how lucky I'd been to find anything at all. Anyway, I'd found a place. It was a tiny little room in a dilapidated clapboard shack, run by an old crone with about three marbles left rolling around in her skull. She was fat and hideously ugly and had a little white beard and mustache. You'd come in the door and she'd come barging out.

"Who the fuck's there?" she'd yell.

At first I'd tell her who it was but after two or three times I just ignored her. The room upstairs had no kitchen, no table, no place to eat, just a bed and a shower and nothing else. I'd never stayed in a place that shitty for any extended amount of time; it made me slightly depressed. But all I had to do was go outside and go wander around near the beach and I immediately perked up. God damn, California shure was purty. The sun shone down and the palm trees swayed in the breeze and everyone looked happy, no one was rushing around or worrying about anything, it really was nice.

The people down the hall were a young couple named Craig and Lizzy. They'd recently done something similar to what I'd done, got in their beat-up old jalopy and fled Illinois and made for the coast. It wasn't just me; California had that effect on people, the fabled laid-back attitude and the beaches and all that. All the hot chicks falling from the trees. Craig had long blonde hair and a muscular physique. He had an entirely dissipated look about him; I don't want to say sleazeball, but since it's the first word that comes to mind I will. He looked like a younger version of those demented letches running around in overcoats flashing all the girls on the street and scaring the bejeezus out of them. It was probably only a few years away. His eyes drooped down and his teeth looked like they'd been filed to points, and he talked as if he were drugged, or at least extremely sleepy. Lizzy was short and squat with frizzy red hair, she wasn't terribly attractive and was constantly pissed off. She made a fair bit of noise and didn't look like someone you wanted to cross, in fact I was almost afraid to talk to her at all. Craig said she liked to dress up like a vampire in her spare time. Upon hearing this, I was even more reluctant to engage - perhaps she'd eat me were we to disagree. What an odd bunch I'd run into out in Cali. It was a bit like living in a circus.

It was strange but it was interesting. Refreshing, exhilarating even, a total mind fuck. Craig and Lizzy and I would go out to the bars and it wasn't like before, somehow it was an adventure now, even though the stools felt the same underneath your ass and the beer tasted the same. We'd get drunk and loose and go wandering around and I'd go into my sign-banging routine and they'd laugh and everything would be alright. The place was crawling with douchebags, but it wasn't getting to me like it had back east. There was something magical about southern California, something charmed, something warm and reassuring. I didn't know how long it would last but for the time being I was more than prepared to just ride the wave, to be led by the winds of fate and go wherever they took me. It was about as far from that cubicle as Jupiter was from Mars, that was all I knew, and all I wanted to know. I felt awakened. The move was already serving its purpose, it was working.

26

Craig came over to the room. "Try some of this, man, it'll really knock you out." He was holding a baggie and a rolled-up dollar bill.

"What is it?"

"It's speed, man."

I'd never tried any before, but what the hell, I was feeling reckless. Fuck everything anyway. I snorted the powder up my nose and felt it go charging around my body. In minutes I was more full of energy than I'd ever been before, a live wire shooting sparks of lightning from everywhere, out my eyes and my ass and everywhere else. We went out to the bars that night and I barely knew what was going on, all I knew was that I was having one hell of a good time.

It went on like that for awhile, weeks, months. Craig was into his drugs and every so often he'd show up with some new stuff he'd gotten from somewhere. I'd never done drugs before and it really threw me for a loop, it messed with my head pretty hard. It was speed for the most part and what it did was it made you feel invincible, like you were fifty feet tall, like you could do anything at all. One night we were at the bar and I was talking to this chick and I leaned over in the middle of the conversation and kissed her, just like that, and the strangest part about it was that she didn't even mind, she just sat there and smiled.

A few weeks later we were in their room, sitting around vegetating after an evening of debauchery. The music was on and the candles were lit and everyone was feeling mellow, stoned. I was assuming it wasn't speed Craig had given me earlier because I was just way too relaxed; it might have been crack, I knew he did that occasionally as well. All night long Craig had been regaling me with his crazy stories of the past. He'd gone to jail once and there'd been this ex-baseball pitcher in the cell with him; to assert himself proactively he'd gotten up to start some trouble and had been knocked on his ass so quick his head had spun.

"Those baseball pitchers have good hands," he said chuckling.

He'd also been going on at length about how he wouldn't mind being a dancer in a gay club, which had me wondering. He said it was the money but I suspected it was probably something else. He was one freaky dude, there was just about nothing he wasn't into. We'd gotten shit-faced drunk a few nights earlier and in an unguarded moment I'd let slip about my own wackiness and he'd sounded rather intrigued, almost too much so. Life was certainly interesting around Craig.

So there we were, sitting around the room. Craig and Lizzy were up on the bed snorting something and I was on the floor, lying on my back. I was pretty well spent, I was done, I wasn't ready for any more excitement. Craig and Lizzy had other ideas. I'd closed my eyes for a second and when I opened them back up again, they were both sitting on the edge of the bed, looking down at me. Craig had a strange lecherous gleam in his eye, I wondered what the hell they were up to.

"Go ahead," he was urging Lizzy, whispering in her ear, almost caressing it with his words.

Lizzy stepped forward onto my chest tentatively, first with one foot, then the other. I closed my eyes again. She trampled me softly like that for a while, gingerly at first, then a little harder, gradually easing herself into it. She was obviously afraid she'd hurt me. I looked up at Craig and saw the sensual little smirk he had on his face, he was getting off on me getting off. And there was Lizzy mincing around on my chest and neck and face leaving little footprints everywhere and me sprawled out like a starfish beneath, just taking it all in, muddled, amazed, in wonder.

When she'd had enough, Lizzy climbed back onto the bed. Now I needed more, I got up and helped myself to another line. I looked at the clock, it said four-thirty. Outside the window, the San Diego night continued on with its breezy hushing self, with the sound of the ocean just off in the distance and the palm trees silhouetted against the moon, stark and ghostly there in the pale light. It was undoubtedly the most surreal night of my life.

27

So the money was already running out. I'd saved up a little but not near enough, and here I was a few weeks in and the ship was leaking so bad it was already in danger of sinking. I figured I'd better at least try to get a job. I'd hooked up a computer in the room and now I made a few halfhearted attempts at poking around and looking for something. I sent out a few resumes and nothing came back, nothing at all, just radio silence, followed by more of the same. I'd only had the one job and hadn't really been doing anything terribly productive at said one job and so the resume was lacking and I knew it. I didn't really want a job anyway so the situation didn't bother me all that much. San Diego was the perfect place to become a bum, the weather was always between sixty-five and eighty-five and there were lots of nice soft sandy places to lay down at night.

While the money ran out, I kept at it with the old novel. I'd sit down at night with the little light on and the little fingers ready to type away and absolutely nothing would happen, it was the same as always, it was just impossible. I tried this, I tried that, I tried writing about Cali and some of the new experiences I'd been having and the results never varied, not one iota. Maybe I needed to let things percolate for a few months, maybe I didn't know the place well enough yet. There was definitely some material to work with: the old crone downstairs and crazy Craig and Lizzy and all the rest. That much was for sure. But another few weeks of stasis and I was thoroughly disgusted. I decided to just put the whole thing down for awhile and go do something else.

I took to walking the streets of Pacific Beach. I went up and back along the avenue, took walks along the beach, went into places to get coffee or beer (beer for the most part). The women were all so beautiful, they were all so fresh and young. At least half of them were blonde and they all had long tanned limbs and wore pretty little sundresses. Each of them as lovely as a flower, each in the prime of life and enjoying it to the fullest, each one of them reserved for someone else. More of the same, everything off limits, everything inaccessible and impossible. There needed to be more exceptions to the rule, I mean in life, in general. Every so often the fates could cut you a break, or could slip up or look the other way so that someone somewhere actually got what he or she wanted. God was a corporate stooge, he believed in a rigged deck.

Now I needed a woman again. All this Cali madness had me in heat, I couldn't just sit there and do nothing. I'd gone back over to Craig and Lizzy's room one night to see if there would be a repeat performance but there wasn't one, all they'd done was sit around and play cards. I caved and decided to go see a domme. They were expensive but a man had needs and there was nothing else to be done. It had been a while since I'd seen one and I was decidedly nervous on the way over, on pins and needles the entire time. The one I was going to see was named Celia. I'd found her on the internet. She was blonde like the rest and looked pretty damn good, although you never could tell from the picture. She'd had icy blue eyes and ruby red lips and had been wearing thigh-high black leather boots and had been holding a leather cat-o-nine-tails in her hand. Her skin had been pale as snow and her sharp nails were as ruby red as her lips. It was enough to drive a man mad.

I found my way to the right address and knocked on the door. I was even more nervous now than before, there was some sweat on my forehead which I'd been wiping away. The door opened and there Mistress Celia stood in all her glory. She opened the door wider and allowed me to enter, then I followed her into the other room. It was a fairly normal little sitting room, with a couch and a few chairs, not really a dungeon of any sort. Some of these places were wild-looking with their whips and racks and thrones and things, you never knew what you'd find when you got there. Mistress Celia seated herself on the couch and pointed down at the floor, to a spot just in front of her. I knelt. Without a word she slapped me across the face.

"You're late," she said. She had me apologize, offered me her hand to kiss and then continued.

"Take your clothes off and put them in a pile, there in the corner. Place the tribute on the table. I'll be right back."

Mistress Celia left the room. I did as bidden. I removed my clothes and put them in a bundle, put the money on the table in a neat little stack and then returned to my previous position. A few minutes later she came back in and reseated herself on the couch. She was just as advertised, she looked good, real good. She wasn't really hot, if we're speaking clinically, not smoking hot like some of the others, but she was just hot enough to make me swoon anyway. Her hair and eyes and nails shone out and blinded me with a lust that was barely containable. She was sleek and smooth and altogether mysterious, and she had that certain quality that some of the dommes had, not all of them, just one every now and then, that arrogant smirk, that delicious smoldering gleam that suggested she was in fact really enjoying this shit, that it wasn't just about the money. I mean let's face it, you basically had to be a bitch to do this job. At least for any considerable length of time.

So there the Goddess sat, on the couch just a few feet away, legs crossed and eyeing me superciliously.

"Remove my shoes," she said.

She was wearing a pair of tall black heels that just about stopped my heart whenever I so much as glanced at them. I slipped them from her feet as instructed. Beautiful, soft feet, all curves and elegant wonder. She placed one on my shoulder rather roughly and pressed the other one into my face.

"Lick my feet," she commanded.

I began running my tongue along the sticky rubbery soles, bathing and worshiping them with my tongue, lapping at them with abandon, like a dog. An act that would have been considered torture by a vast majority of the human race was my own personal idea of heaven, the very reason for my existence, the key to unlock all doors in whatever halls of pleasure existed in this cruel unfeeling world of ours. It was my cross to bear, what could I say. I'd long since stopped questioning it or thinking about it, I just did my thing and life continued on one way or another. First one foot, then the other, then back to the first. I licked Mistress Celia's feet clean for fifteen minutes, twenty, a half an hour, adoring her with abandon, and all the while she was lounging back in the cushions with a hedonistic smile on her face, eyes closed and basking in the attention, all but purring like a cat. A vulgar display of power, to be sure. I supposed it was a good enough gig if you could get it. Not all the time, mind you - some of these guys were into some pretty crazy shit, they wanted pins put into their skin or their balls crushed or whatever the hell else it was. Then again it was probably no worse than having to sit in some factory all day long. Depends on how you look at it, I suppose.

But anyway, the session went on. Mistress Celia had me stop cleaning her feet and then laid me down on the floor and trampled me for awhile, allowed me the obligatory release, collected the money off the table, said goodbye and shut the door behind me. Just like that, it was over. Wham bam thank you Ma'am, next in line please, step right up. I drove home with the sight of her racing around behind my eyes, the smell of her still in my nose, the feel of her cool silky skin against my own, as if she were still right there touching me. Sometimes I felt like it did more harm than good. You left and then she wasn't there anymore and all you did was go get yourself black-out drunk trying to forget it had ever even happened, I mean what was the point. Life was continual torment. I wondered if it had to be that way. You got glimpses sometimes of alternatives; I wasn't sold yet on the inevitability of the whole thing. But for the time being things remained inevitable. Mistress Celia owned my thoughts and dreams that night, and then the next night, and the one after. If anything more spectacular than that had ever been invented in the realm of human experience, I had yet to encounter it. Thank You Mistress Celia, thank You Mistress. Thank you.

28

Craig came by on Friday night, we went out and got drunk. He'd mentioned some reason as to why Lizzy wasn't there but I hadn't really caught it, and not caring much either way I hadn't pressed for clarification. Upon our return we were feeling wild and half out of our minds. Craig asked if I was into porn, I said sometimes. He made me get a tape out and pop it in the machine. It was one of mine, a real specialty item, something that would have been considered outlandish by most other standards. See above. One girl had the other girl down on the floor and was having her way with her, being the bossy little bitch that she was. We ogled the ongoings for a few minutes and then I began to hear slight moaning sounds coming from the vicinity of the floor.

"Ohhhhh, that's so hot..." Craig was moaning.

I looked down and found it exceedingly strange that he was watching me now instead of the tape, out of the corner of his eye but noticeably enough. He wasn't the one into this shit, what the hell was he going on about. He was laying there on the floor grinning like a subnormal and diddling himself ever so slightly and all the while his glances kept straying back over in my direction. I put two and two together in my drunken addled brain and decided that he was hoping I'd start jerking off in front of him so that he could watch. It sounded plausible enough and it would have been right up his alley. I refrained from indulging him however and the moaning quickly stopped.

A few nights later, there came a rapping on the door. I looked at the clock and saw that it was past three in the morning. I got up to answer the door and there Craig was, standing buck naked in the hallway next to some other chick I'd never seen before, a girl with a few extra pounds on her who was also buck naked. Both of them were just standing there, smiling, not saying a word. Aha, more freaky shit, I got it. I mumbled something about being too tired and excused myself, shutting the door in their faces. I wondered where Lizzy had gone, somewhere else I supposed. Or maybe she was in on it and was waiting back at the room. I doubted it though. Her freakiness only ran to a certain point. Evidently it stopped at vampirism.

I lay back down, sinking into the depths of the marshmallowy mattress. It was so pathetically soft it threatened to swallow you whole, you got up in the morning fighting for your freedom. I lay there thinking about things. Craig was all over the place, he was a nut, he was the original wild child. I was definitely getting the feeling he was gay, or at least bi. I speculated on how the threesome would have gone. All of this was new to me, I didn't know how that would have even worked, the logistics of it and such. I considered things further, the wider picture. My life had gotten strange and interesting but there was something unsettling about it all. It had certainly changed direction but I wasn't sure if the new direction was necessarily a better one - more of a lateral movement, I suspected, into a more unconventional space but with the situation generally unimproved. My health certainly wasn't appreciating the new change in scenery, I could tell you that beyond a doubt. We'd been doing way too much speed and there were days afterwards when I really felt like I was going to die, like my head had come loose from its moorings and just wanted to go drifting around the room all by its lonesome. The old brain cells were being eaten up at an unsustainable pace. But I was fairly satisfied anyway with the way things were going. I was living some kind of life, at least, I wasn't just sitting around hiding in my room, waiting for the end. It was better than most of the others could say.

29

I woke up on a Monday morning without a headache for a change. There was a white baggie full of speed sitting there on the nightstand, right next to my head, a little parting gift Craig had left from a few nights earlier. I said screw it and snorted it up, then went into the shower and got myself all nice and squeaky clean. Outside the window the sun was shining, it looked like a nice day out. Now I had plenty of energy, an excess of it, and so to siphon some of it off I decided to go do a little exploring. I hopped in the car and went north along the water, taking residential streets until I reached some sort of amusement area, with a boardwalk, a roller coaster and the whole nine yards. I was high as a kite at this point and so I immediately jumped on the roller coaster, went whooshing around and then got back on for a second ride. The wind went whipping through my hair, my blood was pumping through my veins and I could see the ocean, dipping and weaving off to one side as the little car went up and down, round and round.

I got off the coaster, considered going for a third time then opted to take a stroll along the boardwalk instead. The weather was so nice, it was really beautiful, with everything all blue and gold and not a cloud in the sky. The weather was always nice here, it was almost overkill. It being a Monday there weren't a lot of people around, I had the whole place to myself. Some of the little businesses were open, some of them were closed. I went into a candy shop to get a soda, then upon passing a tattoo parlor dragged myself by the hair and veered inside for a closer look. A fat man with rubber bands in his beard was sitting at the counter watching me. He looked like a hairy frog. His arms and neck and even his face were covered in tattoos, it all just blended together into one big blue-green mess. I'd never gotten a tattoo before, never even considered it really, but there I was looking through the binders and perusing the various options.

"I'll get that one," I said, pointing at a little red and yellow star, a supernova of some sort. "On the shoulder."

The tattoo guy put the supernova on my shoulder and I went back outside. It had hurt a little, but not too bad. The speed was still doing its job. This shit really did make you feel bulletproof, like you could overcome any obstacle, climb any mountain, like you could leap tall buildings in a single bound.

I walked around for another hour or so before heading back. I drove through the ritzy areas, past La Jolla and all that crap, looking at the fancy houses, staring at all the beautiful girls on the street, strutting around like winners of the grand prize, all that self-love, all that smug satisfaction. Another few hours of that and I couldn't think of anything else to do so I just went home. The whole Cali thing was still novel and somewhat exciting, but I was starting to feel like I was just spinning my wheels. The satisfaction I'd been feeling previously had melted away rather quickly and left me with a strange gnawing sense of uncertainty. Not to say I wanted to get a job or anything, mind you, definitely nothing that crazy, just that there wasn't a whole lot of focus and not much of a point. I didn't know if it were even possible to find a point to life, but this new path I'd chosen didn't exactly feel like the road to enlightenment; in fact it was feeling more and more like a dead end, albeit a sunny pleasant one. Things needed to be sustainable, that was the word I'd been using lately, and this didn't fit the bill. It was a transitory phase and I knew it. I didn't know what would come next.

30

So I continued spinning my wheels. I figured I'd try a little sightseeing, see how that went. I drove up to Los Angeles, where things were all plastic and fake, full of smog and overcrowded as hell. They were all trying to pretend they were in Hollywood up there, the waitresses, the cabbies, the friggin' janitors, it was pretty damned goofy if you asked me. I went across to Las Vegas, where all they wanted to do was gamble, it was like a big hole in the desert to throw your money into. I could throw my money away easily enough without having the hole dug for me, thank you very much. I drove up the coast, through Santa Barbara, past the Hearst Castle, past Big Sur, through the tall trees and along the winding roads all the way up to Frisco; I went up and down hills and saw fog and hung out in the seedier end of town, the Tenderloin they called it. All the homeless and freaks and assorted maniacs running wild in the street, shooting up and chasing each other around in circles and banging pots and pans on the ground and things, like a warzone, downright surreal. I hung out in the dive bars for a few nights and it was more of the same, just a bunch of wackos and degenerates getting drunk and making very little sense. At night the hookers and junkies came out and went prowling around, lurking in the shadows, hissing and menacing, asking you for your money or your life or whatever the hell else it was they wanted. A sea of malcontents in all directions, no end in sight. The desperation got to me after awhile and so I pulled up stakes and retreated south, heading back the way I'd come. The world was truly messed up, beyond description, beyond belief. You went looking for signs of betterment but there weren't any, not anywhere; one coast was just as good as another. At least that was how I felt about it. I'd been in California close to three months already and I hadn't seen jack shit that suggested to me they had any more of a clue out there than we had back home. They had sunshine, fine, there was that. But sunshine wasn't enough, and neither were palm trees. The place was wearing on me and I was all alone and I didn't know how much longer I was going to last.

I went out and tried to do things. Having decided that Craig and Lizzy were just a little too much trouble, I'd started venturing out on my own on the weekends, hitting the bars and such, back to the old routine, sitting on barstools drinking by myself. The old malaise returned with a vengeance, it was the same old shit all over again. I was gun shy by myself and found it impossible to talk to people, and they sensed my unease and responded in the predictable fashion, with turned backs and cold shoulders, persona non grata, see ya later and don't let the door hit you on the way out. This had all been so much easier back in college. I missed Will, more than anything else, I missed his company, missed how human he made me feel. I sat there commingling with all those insincere plastic fakeos, lounging in their comfy chairs under their pretty lights, slapping each other on the back and drowning in their sea of status-obsessed money-grubbing living death and all I could think of was going down the street and plunging myself into the ocean. Everywhere you went, this was all there was. All that could even be considered. The thought of it was too mind-numbing for words; I reeled, I staggered, I fought for breath. I stumbled out onto the street to get some fresh air, there, I could breathe better again. The sun blazed down on me like the wrath of the gods, like the vengeance of Apollo, it pounded down like the end of days. Down the street and over a few blocks and there was the beach. I sat there in the sand for hours, for what felt like forever, arms on knees and head bowed, I sat there until the sun went down and all the people were gone. All those people with their happy eyes and flashing smiles and easy carefree ways, none of whom appeared to feel like I did. I wondered what was wrong with me. I wondered what there was to do. I couldn't bring myself to go back into another bar, so I went back to my room instead. The landlady came out to challenge me, I returned fire, cursing her out. Up the stairs and inside. Now it was the room's turn to assault me; it was such a tiny space, it lay on top of me, wrapped itself around my neck, crushed my lungs like some insidious consumptive disease. A little dead end inside a bigger one. It was no longer working. The dream was all but dead. The dream was dead and there was nowhere else to go. Mexico? What the hell was I going to do in Mexico. Who knew, perhaps there was no place for me in America or Mexico or anywhere else, maybe no place for me in the entire world. If I fled the planet in a spaceship and wound up on Venus or Mars, I'd probably get the same reception. It was a problem of galactic proportions.

After a few days of just aimlessly wandering around, I wound up back at the beach. I was finding that you wound up there no matter what you tried to do, it was just inevitable here. I sat myself down on the low concrete wall and had a look around. A bum was standing there next to me, rummaging through his shopping cart. He was a big black guy who looked around fifty years old or so. Maybe a bit older, hard to tell. It was nice and warm out but he was wearing a big heavy jacket anyway, some army surplus thing. He probably didn't want to get it stolen or something.

"How ya doin'," I said. I had nothing better to do. I waited to see what he'd do; either he'd hit me or he'd start up a conversation.

"Doin' okay, thanks," he said.

The latter, apparently. I took a closer look at him. He was real grizzled, with white stubble for a beard and thick weathered skin that looked like it had seen a few too many summers in the Sahara Desert (or the Mojave at the very least). I waited to see if he'd say anything further but he just kept rummaging through all the stuff he had there piled up in the cart. It appeared he was looking for something he'd misplaced.

"Where ya from?" I asked.

"Fargo, North Dakota," he crisply replied.

"Wow, a long way from home, eh?" Figured I'd throw in some Canadian, make him feel more at ease. They spoke Canadian up there.

"Yep," he said. "A long ways from home."

"How'd ya wind up here?"

"Long story."

"I got time." I smiled.

"Welp, I won't bore ya with all the damn details. But less jest say I been around the wheel a few times. I seen more o' this country of ours than any man livin'. I'd be willing to swear by it, I would."

"You been around, eh?"

"Yessir, I have."

"Where was the best place you been to?"

"Didn't like any of em."

"Damn, sorry to hear."

"It's a cold, cruel world, son."

I glanced back over at him expecting to find him looking all bitter, but instead he was wearing a strange sort of wry grin, as if he knew something the rest of us didn't. He looked wise.

I went dark. I agreed with him but didn't feel the need to say it. Now he himself went from curt to receptive.

"Where you from, son?"

"I'm from New Jersey."

"What brought you out to California?"

"I don't know."

I half expected a chuckle but he just smiled; he understood what I was saying.

"Sometimes you jes gotta get out and see things fo yoself," he declared.

"Even though it's a cold cruel world," I agreed.

"Thass right, even though. Or maybe even because of it. If no place works fo you, then you gotta try someplace else."

"But you have to stop eventually. You have to land somewhere."

"I suppose you do."

"Is this the end of the line for you?"

"I suppose it is."

"Why?"

"The weather's nice. I kin sleep at night and not freeze myself bout half to death."

"Fargo's pretty damn cold, eh?"

"You damn straight it is."

I sat there with the old feller for quite some time, watching the sun drift across the cloudy sky. Yep, there were clouds for once. Every so often it threatened to rain here. I sat with my newfound companion and weighed him against all the others there and decided I'd rather spend the afternoon with him than anyone else. And so I did. We sat there in relative silence, with just the occasional observation or aside, watching the goings-on and feeling the breeze against our faces, and things felt all right for a change, things felt sane. They had to drive you almost into the ground before you approximated anything human. Or maybe the ones who started out that way were the ones destined to wind up there the fastest. We sat there for a good long spell, the old-timer and I, and then after a few hours he got up and said he had to go, grabbed ahold of his shopping cart and shambled off down the boardwalk. Never even got his name. I watched him slowly recede into the distance. He had a touch of grace to him, something dignified, almost refined. I decided that he'd been a prince among paupers, and I determined to go have a drink in his honor. I went into the first place I came across, an outdoor bar with the terrace and the fans and all the rest, and I sat myself down at the bar and ordered a beer. The bartender didn't like the looks of me, I was looking a little rough around the edges, I wasn't wearing the right fucking clothes or something. I didn't care, it didn't even get through this time, I ordered the beer and smiled, smiled at him when he put it down in front of me, smiled as he walked away, smiled all the way through drinking it, smiled as I ordered another one. His response was invalid. It had just been demonstrated that the world in fact wasn't just for them. There were others of us too, others that mattered, and although the whole world could shit on us all it wanted, we were still there, we existed, we objected, and we were capable of providing each other with a modicum of support, at least every now and then, as the opportunity presented itself. The world didn't care about us, no matter how much they tried to pretend it did when we were younger, all us outcasts and misfits and weirdos, all us bums and derelicts and dropouts, it didn't care about us at all, whether we lived or died or made it or didn't make it or any other damn thing; we were expendable, loose parts, odds and ends scattered upon the great scrapheap of life, but maybe we could care about each other instead and that would be good enough, that would be something, that would be okay. Maybe it was enough to live on, maybe enough to get by. I damn sure hoped it would be. I blocked the bartender from my sight and spent the remainder of the early evening focusing on the memory of my new friend. I felt like I'd make it through the next few hours, if nothing else.

31

There was a movie theatre down at the other end of the main drag, and on a whim I went in. It was a weekday and early in the afternoon, the matinee session, things were quiet and I was just about the only one there. I sat in the dark with my popcorn and watched. I had no idea what I was even watching, I'd picked the movie entirely at random but the more I watched the more it drew me in. The story was pretty interesting, it was about teenage angst, about a kid like me who was stuck in his life, just running around all the time like a chicken with his head cut off, getting nowhere fast. His parents were morons and his friends weren't much better and the job sucked and yadda yadda, all the same stuff I was well familiar with, the chicks he couldn't have, the places he'd never go, the life he'd never lead. In the beginning it was intriguing but after about an hour it had become disturbing and I couldn't make it through the whole thing, I had to get up and leave it was bothering me so much. I went outside the theatre and stood on the sidewalk. Brilliant sunlight again. The sun was getting offensive; it was always there, trying to blind you, wilting you into submission, crippling you with its beauteousness. I'd been here too long already.

I went down the street until I came to a laundromat. I went in there, just to get out of the sun. There were a couple of old ladies in the corner sifting through big piles of clothes, and another younger one sitting watching the dryer spin round. She had dark hair tied in a ponytail and she was wearing shorts and a t-shirt. I thought about what it would be like to talk to her. I thought about what it would be like to talk to anybody. I hadn't done it in awhile; the more I thought about it the more I realized it really had been quite a long time. A week went by and you hadn't opened your mouth once. Craig and Lizzy were off doing their own thing and I was letting them, I was just kind of sick of all the drama and bullshit. Besides, as wacky as Craig was, I'd been getting the sneaking feeling that he was eventually going to land me in jail if I hung out with him too often. So it was me and the world, again. Me and the big bad monolithic world, mano a mano. No Will to stand alongside. I missed the crazy bugger. I'd have to write him a letter or give him a call or something to see how he was doing. I hadn't talked to my folks in months either, I resolved to give them a call and then immediately reversed the decision. It would just end in trouble. I was tired of trouble all the time. You didn't even have to go looking for it, it found you either way. Cosmic informants on every corner, pointing the bastard in the right direction. More conspiracies abounding.

After the laundromat I thought about getting in the car and driving around some, but then reconsidered. I didn't really see the point, all you did was get snagged in traffic and sit there in the smog waiting to suffocate. The last time I'd tried it, I'd almost rear-ended the guy in front of me at a light because the girl walking down the street had her skirt so short. So there were other dangers as well. Danger, danger everywhere, perilous pitfalls, distractions in skirts, turmoil in drag, snarling traffic and brilliant sunlight and landladies demanding rent and the police ready to pounce every time you went out your door and goddamnit if this world didn't have its head so firmly up its own ass there was no hope of reclaiming it. There had to be something you could do, but for the life of me I just couldn't see it. What pissed me off the most was that I had a good head on my shoulders, I knew it, I was supposed to have figured this shit out by now and yet I was constantly being flummoxed and baffled and pummeled and batted around all over the place, just defeated at every turn. But there was a way out. There had to be. And if there wasn't, I was going to make one. I'd dig a tunnel to China if I had to, stow away on a ship and take a slow boat to Buenos Aires, sail off to Greenland and make like an eskimo. I'd jump off a bridge if it got to be too much. I simply was not prepared to accept what they were insisting was true. There was more, goddamnit, there was more.

32

I took another weak stab at the novel but found myself writing about Tracey and so I stopped. Then that night I had another dream about her, the first one in weeks. I couldn't even remember what had happened when I woke up, I just knew it had been about her. I felt like shit for another few days and then one day when I was sitting at the computer I typed her name into the search bar just to see what would come up. I knew I wasn't supposed to be doing it, and yet there I was, doing it. I couldn't help myself. Nothing came back except a long list of other people I didn't recognize; I supposed that wasn't exactly a surprise considering the fact that Wilson was a pretty damn common name. I was simultaneously relieved and disappointed. I didn't know what I thought I was going to do with the information, even had I been able to acquire it. My mind was an inconstant foolish thing.

And into that inconstant foolish thing I collapsed. I lay in bed and did nothing at all for days, sprawled myself out flat on my back and flatlined. I went cave-diving, spelunking, seeking out lost threads, pearls of mental residue, little things that had gotten lost in there and refused to come out. The dorm rooms up on North Campus, all warm and snuggly and cozy, full of friends gathered there to chat. Cathy, Marie, George, Pedro. Basketball games in high school, long lazy afternoons spent on the courts out along that stretch of busy main road. The sound of laughter. Other things long forgotten, flickering fragments of memory. Meeting Will for the first time. My little brother Jake's beaming face when he won that award in grade school, the essay-writing contest, when he'd gone up there on stage to all that applause and had his picture taken for the local paper. He couldn't have been more than eleven or twelve, fifth grade, sixth at the most. My mother when she was younger, when she'd occasionally flare up and burst into life, laughing and singing like she still enjoyed doing the things she did, before the years got to her and made her into what she was today. Happier times, simpler times. Peace on Earth. The things you did during the day made sense, they had specific purpose, you knew exactly why you were doing these things, and as a result it felt good to do them. Dancing eyes, soft smiles, merriment all around. My own eyes finding things to thrill them, to provide them with joy, little snapshots of gold and silver, now tarnished and faded. Where had it all gone. I tried to remember the last time I'd felt good, like really good, like it had been back in college, and I couldn't come up with anything, all I knew was that it had been years ago. There were so many years left, so much space to fill, so much time to kill. Jesus Christ, what a joke.

Finally I got my ass up and resumed my life. I went down to the convenience store to get myself some food. One needed to eat now and then. That was in fact one of the things you could do to pass the time. I bought a pair of those rancid hot dogs they have at those places, you know, the ones on the chrome rods that look like they've been sitting there broiling away for like three days (and probably have). I took the hot dogs outside with me and wolfed them down. I immediately felt worse than before. Everything was a trap, we were constantly being waylaid. I was sick of it. Even the hot dogs threatened you. On the way out of the store a Mexican gangster dude wanted to start some trouble, I'd apparently gotten too close to him, or at least that was the excuse he was choosing to use. I ignored him and he left me alone. He had a do-rag on and his pants hanging down and all the rest and he was making all sorts of noise. I supposed that was another way of passing the time.

33

California may have been all sunshine and beaches but it was also violent. I was coming back from the store one day when I saw Craig standing in the middle of the street, shouting at someone in the doorway of the apartment house. He had his shirt off and was irate, he was screaming and yelling like a loon.

"Meet me halfway, Gary! Meet me halfway!" he was shouting.

Gary was another guy who was staying with us in the house, he was the one standing in the doorway. He was some lowlife I'd only talked to like once or twice. Craig was standing there flexing his manly muscles and strutting back and forth, trying to draw Gary out into a fight. Not having talked to Craig in a while, I had no idea what it was all about. Probably either money or women. Or both. Whatever it had been, it was strange seeing someone standing in the middle of the street like that threatening to do violence; I couldn't remember ever having seen it before.

Then a few days later when I came back home, Craig was crouched in the bushes just outside the door. I asked him what the hell he was doing.

"It's Lizzy, man, she's out there. She's looking for me."

"What?"

"Yeah, we had another fight, she started banging her head on the wall again. It got pretty ugly this time. She's throwing shit at me and we're going back and forth and the next thing I know she's saying she's gonna kill me and I'm running outside to get away from her. You don't know what she's like when she gets like this, man. She's fuckin' crazy, I'm tellin' ya. Like crazy for real."

His droopy eyes weren't drooping nearly as much as usual, I could almost see them for a change. He was more fired up than I'd ever seen him, just quivering like a leaf. Before I could say anything else, I saw their old jalopy crawling down the street towards us. Lizzy was driving along real slow with her shades on, surveying the terrain, looking this way and that. I could see her lips moving, she was talking a blue streak to herself.

"Oh shit," Craig said. "Get down, hide."

I hunkered down next to him in the bushes and we waited. The car drove slowly by. I could feel the tension pulsing from him, from a few feet away, could sense the panic, could see the sweat dripping down his face. This chick had really put the fear of God into him, he was completely spooked. Vampires were serious business.

So southern Cali wasn't all wine and roses, there was some heavy shit going on there as well. Trouble in paradise, like they said. I don't know why it surprised me but it did. I mean the place was so damn beautiful and yet there they were, out in the streets trying to tear each other limb from limb, like they had no choice in the matter and were compelled to do it. It appeared that no place on Earth was safe from the folly of the human experience. Everywhere you went, it was the same barely glossed-over mess. The desperation just rose up from the pavement, like vaporous filth, everything reeked of it.

You'd see all the yuppies and Barbies and Kens wandering around on the street going in and out of the restaurants and bars and living the high life and then you'd go another few blocks inland and it all collapsed - bums and winos, bag ladies and welfare mothers, hard-luck cases for miles, just a big unending sea of them. Everyone looked haunted, harried, like prey being hunted for their pelts, clothes in rags, shoes falling apart, big white eyeballs throwing terrified glances over hunched shoulders like the devil himself was following close behind, half of them looking like they had no place to stay for the night. For every so-called winner there were at least a thousand losers. They'd been at this society thing for thousands of years now and they hadn't progressed any further than this, it was a farce. I figured at a certain point you had to just declare it a failed experiment and start over again from scratch, go back to the trees and start swinging from vines again and eating berries and seeds. I sat and thought about it for a few days to digest it further, to see if maybe I'd been overreacting, but I hadn't been; nothing changed, it was plain as day what I was seeing with my own eyes right there in front of me. There was nothing more to see, the whole thing was a lost cause, and as such one place was just as good as another. It added fuel to the fire, reinforced the conclusion I'd already drawn, that things had just about run their course out there and that it was time for me to be moving on. I didn't want to stay but I didn't want to go. Damned if I did and damned if I didn't. Out of the frying pan and into the fire. The grass is always greener on the other side. Pick a cliché and run with it, any old one you wanted. There were so many different ways to say you were fucked.

34

Another month went by. I was running out of money. I was mired in tedium, swimming in ennui. I'd long since run out of things to do, but that part of it didn't really bother me too much - doing nothing was still better than doing something that actively tortured you. I hadn't tried writing the novel in awhile. It felt good not to be trying to write it. I didn't mind doing other things.

I'd pretty much been relegated to sitting around the room drinking beer, that was what I spent most of my time doing. I sat there listening to the walls breathe, eavesdropping on the sounds of silence. Every so often I'd hear something else. Like the night I was sitting in my room imbibing and the Mexicans next door were having dust-up, they were really going at it, banging and crashing around. I heard a woman scream and a few doors slam and then the screams got even louder; I assumed she was being beaten up. Another night there was a whole lot of honking in the street with all the cars going by and lots of yelling and cheering. Apparently their baseball team had just won some big game. Whoop de doo.

The hours weighed on me. The nights were darker still. Tracey's ghost had reappeared after a brief hiatus and was back to her old tricks, chasing me around more than ever, I could barely get a moment's rest. My existence had stalled out. I couldn't take a step in any direction. The heavens had been harnessed, the stars were tethered and the whole tied-up strangulated mess was dragging me down. West coast was east coast was the moon for all I cared. Sunshine be damned, I couldn't stay there anymore, not another day longer. It was time to go.

35

I packed my stuff up, threw it in the car, said goodbye to Craig and turned the car around, pointing it east this time. Just like that, no second thoughts, no nothing, I was going home again. I wasn't upset or anything, not really, more disappointed than anything else. The dream had finally died, I'd heard the death rattle and now it was no more.

I decided to take my time on the way back. After all I had nothing better to do, and there the whole country was, sprawled out in front of me like a big welcoming pancake; might as well see some of it whilst passing through. I set out due east, going through the desert. The desert was hot and yellow and ominous. It looked like it meant to kill you. I came to Yuma, proceeded into Arizona. I went through Gila Bend, Red Rock, places with interesting names and absolutely nothing in them, a tumbleweed or two, maybe a gas station if you were lucky. I went through Tucson. It was too hot and I didn't stop, I was afraid my car would melt right into the pavement, fuse with it and become a permanent fixture of the landscape. I rocketed on through the brown featureless terrain. So much for taking my time.

A day or two later I was driving along the Rio Grande, with Texas on my left and Mexico on my right. For some reason I'd never made it down to Tijuana when I'd been out there in Cali and it was bothering me, so I figured I'd compensate for the missed opportunity and check out Juarez when I made it to El Paso, hop across the border and do a little poking around. I pulled into El Paso, found myself a rat trap motel to throw the stuff down, slept the night and then the following morning I went across. No problems at Checkpoint Charlie, just waltz on through. Reverse direction might be more interesting.

Juarez was dry and dusty. It felt like a real border town, like a place on the old western frontier, a bit like the end of the world really. I walked down the Avenida until I came to a little square with tables and sat myself down at one of them. A senorita came to give me a cerveza. Check out my Spanish. All around the square the traffic was swarming, big angry snarls of it kicking up all sorts of dust and debris. Brown-skinned girls were walking by on the sidewalk with sacks balanced on their heads; kids scampered here and there, coming perilously close to the oncoming wheels, oblivious to the danger, dodging dexterously in the tumultuous afternoon swelter. Dogs moved about, striding with purpose, well-accustomed to the mess. I watched as a skinny guy in rags lifted up a sewer grate and deposited a plastic bag full of liquor bottles into the space below, then replaced the grate and kept on walking. At the table next to me was a big fat gringo with a gun holstered to his belt. The wild west was still alive and kicking, you just had to go a bit further south to see it. Wild, man, wild.

The gringo at the table was drunkenly calling for more cerveza. He was the bigwig, the fat cat, the big man, the one who could do whatever he wanted, just because. He had a senorita on each fat flabby thigh, each of whom looked more miserable than the other. The wait staff were catering to his every need, however; he obviously had some money. Or maybe it was just the gun. Now he was hooting and hollering and caterwauling like an idiot, and so I drank down the remnants of my beer and continued on in search of other less stressful diversions. I came to a music club of some sort, a big, cavernous space partially open to the outside. It was too early in the evening, no one else was in there besides the bartender but I went in anyway. I stood with my back to the bar and drank by myself. I felt sad. The bartender came over and gave me a pat on the back.

"Happy, happy, is Mexico!" he said.

The encouragement didn't help. I went further down the street until suddenly a loud cantina was blaring on my right. I went in like a moth drawn to a flame. The place was packed, as in jammed solid with bodies, sardines in human form; I squeezed in the best I could and ordered another beer. It was a real local place, they didn't want the gringos in there. I sat there trying not to explode, just letting the deafening music course painfully back and forth between the two poles of my ears, then I polished off my beer and got the hell out of there before I went insane.

It got dark. I got steadily drunker. I wound up in a pool hall, another place strictly for the locals, but these didn't seem to mind my being in there, at least not to any obvious degree. One of them came over and offered to shoot a few games. I obliged. I eyeballed the locals as the opportunity presented itself. Little guys with dark skin and beady black eyes, wearing blue jeans and boots, some of them with sombreros on their heads. Oily black hair, straight little black mustaches. Drinking their drinks, looking fairly unconcerned with anything and everything. I decided they were all right, I drank a few more beers, shot a few more games. My buddy spoke a few words of English, we chatted back and forth, it was nice.

Things were going well enough until I got outside. The chill evening air hit me in the face and suddenly I realized how drunk I was. I reached into my pocket like a fool to go sorting through the money I had there, right in full view of the local wildlife. One of them came running up and tried to take the money from me. He got ahold of a twenty and I was refusing to let it go; presently there was a ripping sound and then the little fucker was scampering off. I supposed we each now had a ten. Good for him, let him have his ten. See what he could do with it.

I was rip-roaring drunk, and now I was good and mad on top of it. I returned to the border, howling at the moon, dragging my body along behind me like some drunken maimed iguana. Upon reaching the border I pulled the old pull-yourself-together-at-the-last-minute trick and after some lengthy sizing up, the big militant bastard let me through. Back to the rat trap motel with my dissipated gringo ass to pass out properly. I needed to be removed from circulation, I really did. Probably needed to be removed from the gene pool as well.

The rest of the trip went far less eventfully. I stopped in Austin, saw the Alamo, went to San Antonio, walked along the river walk. Sizzled in the laser beam Texas heat. God damn it was hot down here, you could fry an egg on your forehead if you so chose. It felt too hot to live any sort of normal life, at least for six months out of the year or whatever it was. Through Houston, on into New Orleans, to frolic along Bourbon Street and be amongst the idiots. Drunken tourists behaving badly on purpose, what a treat. Like the world needed more of this. A couple of death-defying hangovers later and I'd made it to Atlanta. Nothing to see there, just more heat and smog and traffic. Been there done that, have visited Los Angeles recently. Been driving too long now, almost there, almost there. South Carolina, North Carolina, too many Carolinas. Too much of the damn south. A straight shot up the eastern seaboard through our glorious equally-traffic-infested nation's capital and the next day I was back in Jersey again. Jersey and I had had our differences over the years, but the place really did feel like home. The Turnpike and the Parkway and the bridges and tunnels, the malls and the traffic, the whole damn thing. I drove straight to my parents' house, crawled into their spare bedroom and slept for about twenty-four hours. That being insufficient, I slept for twenty-four more. I couldn't rest enough, couldn't get enough sleep. I was prepared to sleep out the rest of the year if need be.

36

It was depressing being back. Here I was thinking that California or whatever the hell I'd find out there was going to magically solve all my problems, and it hadn't solved a single one of them, it hadn't even made a dent. I'd gone traipsing out there like a conquering hero ready to embrace my new destiny and all I'd gotten was a kick in the teeth and a long ride back home. A few months of nothing but confusion, more muddied water slipping under the bridge. I hadn't taken a single step forward. Might have even gone backward, with the way I felt, might have done some lasting damage to my head. I felt trapped, with nowhere to go next.

So things were back to normal. There had been a development while I'd been away though, Jake had finally moved out and gotten his own place. Mom said he wasn't talking to anyone, which wasn't really anything new. I asked her how he was doing and she said the same, if not worse. I was going to have to go over there and see for myself, see how the brooding little fucker was.

I moped and paced around my parents' house for a few weeks and then got myself another apartment, this one way out in the sticks. Things had gotten expensive these days and I couldn't afford anything else, not without a job or a fat wad of money under the mattress or something like that. The apartment was about a half hour's drive from Morristown but it felt like the end of the road, the line beyond which nothing existed except trees and more trees and a few hicks sprinkled in for good measure. Institutional apartment complexes, row upon row of brick-lined despair, old wooden shacks all slanted and leaning every which way, huddled there in the woods like sullen refugees, like escaped convicts, people driving to the supermarket and back all day long and never anywhere else, a modern wasteland, a real disaster. The last outpost before the void. This place made San Diego look like the utopia to end all utopias. The town had exactly one bar and it was a run-down thing, on its last legs, just barely holding on, and if you tried to go in there on a Friday or Saturday night the cops were sitting in the parking lot waiting to pick you off as you tried to make it back home. There was a big lake right off the main road but you couldn't even get to it unless it was within a certain time window, and even then you had to pay for the privilege - the stars had to be aligned, you needed a note from the governor, the whole nine yards, all the usual bullshit. Everything off limits, the land of liberty, 'land of the free' where nothing was possible. What a joke. The people here were drinking the Kool-Aid. Right along with the rest of the world. Well, over half of them, at least. Three quarters, maybe. I didn't know the exact percentage but I could tell it was a lot.

So I had a roof over my head, but not much else. I didn't have to put up with my parents anymore but there was nowhere to go, and nothing to do. Like I said it was only a half hour's drive to Morristown but with the traffic on Route 80 the way it was, it might as well have been a hundred miles or more, it might as well have been California again. And New York, forget about it, it would take you the rest of your life to get in there. There was a train that went in from somewhere but that just looked like another big hassle with no parking and all the rest and so I didn't even bother to investigate further. If I'd felt trapped before, I felt locked in place now, manacled and strapped into the chair, waiting for the switch to be thrown. There appeared to be only one direction in which you could go; things went from bad to worse, never the other way around. The conspiracies deepened. I was beginning to curse the mother that had birthed me.

I was now obligated to get a job. I went on the internet and promptly found one; for some reason it was a lot easier to do here than in San Diego. I didn't question why, I didn't do that too much anymore, all that mattered was that I had a job again. It was remarkably similar to the last one, in fact it was almost identical, I practically couldn't tell the difference. The keyboard was the same and the mouse was the same and the chair and the cubicle and it was about the biggest dose of deja-vu I'd ever had. The boss was different though. This time it was a big fat guy who was never around. His name was Terry and he was actually quite nice, all jolly and complacent and pleasant in a fat-guy sort of way, but I never really got the chance to talk to him as he was constantly in meetings or locked away in his office or off on the moon or wherever it was. I never saw Terry and no one ever gave me anything to do. I had no idea why in the hell they'd hired me. Perhaps I was a tax write-off or something like that. Honestly it felt okay being a tax write-off, relative to the available alternatives, that is. I sat around with my feet up all morning long, pretended to look at the screen every now and then, took a nice long leisurely lunch, read a book, went back and put my feet up for another few hours and that was it, the whistle blew and I was on the way home again. I never talked to anyone and no one ever talked to me. The whole thing was quite simple. It was staggeringly boring and tedious and soul-stealing but it wasn't too terribly draining, in a physical sense, as long as you didn't mind shutting down and going dark for eight hours a day, as long as that sort of thing didn't bother you too much. My life had even less meaning than ever before, but I was making money again which meant I could buy food and pay rent and remain relatively unthreatened in general, and I supposed that would have to do, at least for the time being. Once more I was resigned to my fate. It was my default state.

37

The nights were long out there at the end of the world. I needed a chick again, and bad, but I really didn't want to go back to the bars, I didn't want to go through all that crap again. I went in circles round the room for weeks at a time, my frustration brewing like bad coffee; I tried watching TV, tried surfing the internet, I tried going outside and looking at the stars, but nothing helped. Now that I was back in the area, my thoughts kept stubbornly drifting to Christine, my old boss, of all people. Now that we weren't working together, was there any chance? Nah, I was dreaming, she wanted nothing to do with me. I was bad meat, I was the last thing she wanted, she'd rather make it with farm animals, she'd commit suicide before going with me. And yet the mere possibility wouldn't leave me alone, would give me no peace, just the renewed proximity alone charged me with a nervous energy that left me positively climbing the walls at night.

I surrendered to my mental problems and determined to find out one way or the other, once and for all. Let her punch me in the face for all I cared, but I was going to actually do something for a change. There was a place around the corner from the old office where I knew she went from time to time, a cafe of sorts where you could get coffee and lunch. I started going down there on weekends and casing the joint, sitting there on stakeout for hours at a time, primarily over lunch but sometimes in the mornings as well. For a couple of weeks nothing happened and then suddenly there she was, going in and then coming out with a coffee in her hand and sitting down on the little streetside patio to drink it. It was cold out, it being late October, but the sun was shining and it wasn't too bad as long as the clouds held off, which they were for the time being. She was sitting there, looking as semi-violent as ever. She always looked angry, even when she was completely at rest. They had a term for the condition these days, 'Resting Bitch Face' they called it. Christine had it, and she had it in spades, she'd really mastered the thing. Just the sight of her gave me fits, it instantly riled me all up. I tried taking a few deep breaths and quickly the deep breaths morphed into near hyperventilation and so I stopped with the deep breaths and just tried to calm myself down without them. How the hell was I going to act casual whilst in the middle of a fit, it just wasn't possible. But I had to do something. For once I wasn't just going home with my tail between my legs. Failure was an option, not trying wasn't. They could arrest me if they wanted, I was going in.

So, eschewing the deep breathing routine, I gathered the few ounces of composure that remained accessible to me and walked across the street, going right over to sit at the table next to her.

"Well, look who it is," I said, sounding surprised. "Fancy running into you here..."

Christine looked over, startled. "Jim! What are you doing here?"

"Oh, I come here from time to time," I said.

She frowned, she knew it was bullshit. If I came here from time to time, she would have noticed by now.

"What have you been up to?" she asked.

"I went out to California for a while. Didn't work out so great and so I came back again," I said.

"That's right, I remember that. You said you were going out there."

She stopped talking, took another little sip of her coffee, turned slightly away. The frown had stuck in place, it wasn't going anywhere. She didn't want me there, I could see that, it was painfully obvious, this was all just an obligation for her. I was distracting her from her normal Resting Bitch Face activities.

"Are you going to get anything?" she asked. More skepticism.

"Oh, yeah, " I said brightly. "Almost forgot."

I went inside, got myself a coffee and returned with it. I thought about asking if she minded me joining her, but the tables were pretty small and I could talk to her just fine from where I was. I supposed it would have been too obvious of a tell.

"So how are things at work?" I asked.

"Oh, the same as always. Things never really change there."

More sipping, more irritated glancing around. Just waiting for me to go away. I didn't care. It was like I wanted her to murder me. Showtime.

"You know, Christine, I... well, I guess I have a confession to make. I always kind of liked you, you know, I don't know if you knew that or not, if you could tell, but in any event, I was thinking that maybe you might want to go grab a drink or something like that some time?"

My voice was quivering and the delivery was way too timid, almost as if I were begging for mercy in advance. There was a short pause, and then she burst out laughing, she actually laughed, right in my face. It looked like she'd made some sort of effort to stifle it at first but I couldn't be sure.

"Are you serious?"

She was still giggling, wasn't putting her hand to her mouth or anything like that, not overly concerned with hiding anything at all. The blood rushed to my head and for a split second I thought I was going to throw the coffee at her, just fire it forward into her face and douse her with hot scalding liquid and see how she liked that, see if she could still laugh with a faceful of hot coffee. I mean, there was bitch and then there was this. She must have seen the flash in my eyes because finally her tone changed, she wasn't necessarily scared but now for whatever reason she felt compelled to make amends, some lame placating comment or two if nothing else. She began to speak but I was already up and running, my feet carrying me further and further away with every passing second. I heard the words trailing after me.

"I'm sorry, but, Jim, I really don't think..."

I found a park and sat down on a bench. I still had the coffee in my hand, so I figured I'd drink it. A few sips later I'd calmed down some. I was rebounding quite well, I thought; in the past this kind of shit would have absolutely floored me. There was always tonight, however. I figured it was going to haunt me for quite some time, no matter what I did or didn't do. I'd been through the wringer before, that was for sure. I considered the whole fiasco further. If I'd known in advance that she was going to react that way, I would have insulted her instead, maybe gotten a free slap across the face for my efforts. Maybe I could have insulted her afterwards. Or maybe she was still there and I could go back and insult her now. No, I'll bet she was gone already. You always thought of these things after it was too late.

So I sat in the park for an hour and watched all the nothingness. The place was fairly loud with all the traffic rushing by, and yet it was deathly still. I watched the people go in and out of the bakery across the street, watched a crow hop around in the grass, watched the cop on the corner direct traffic. It appeared the light was out. A mother wandered through the park with a child, that was it. The world had been doing this kind of thing for thousands of years. It had been the same right from the beginning, there'd never been anything to do, all you could do was sit in parks and fields and observe all the nothingness. That bitch, though. My God, was it eating at me now. I resolved to go gay at the next available opportunity. I didn't like men but I had a feeling things would go better with them than with the so-called fairer sex. I didn't see anything fair about them, not in the slightest.

38

I was back in Philly, visiting Will. It felt so good to see him again I wanted to give him a big hug. Him not being the hugging type, I resisted however. I felt a sense of relief in being able to claim that I still had at least one remaining friend in life. We went out on Friday night and got rip-roaring drunk and it was just like nothing had ever happened, like I'd never gone anywhere, like no beats had been skipped at all. Whee hoo, let the good times roll.

On Saturday Will took me on a long bike ride. Besides going on forced marches, this was the other thing he liked to do, he liked to bike all over town and go pedaling around all day long for no good reason. It always felt like something of a near-death experience dodging through all that traffic and barely missing pedestrians and curbs and signposts, but I hadn't died yet so I figured there was no need to ·object. It was as good a thing to do as any, I supposed. We biked here, we biked there, we biked everywhere. In between rides we stopped for beers.

Eventually we got to the pool hall and paused for more of an extended rest, and to shoot some stick. This place was one of our absolute favorite haunts, we went in whenever we could. It was dark and cavernous and had a series of different rooms with about fifty tables between them, like a cathedral for pool, really a sight to see. And the regulars here took the game seriously; you'd see them hunched over their tables with furrowed brows, looking all grave and concerned, surveying the terrain, seeking out their next shot, worried about leaving the other guy with anything too usable. Old men in suspenders with paunches and long-since receded hairlines, old-timers with a barrelful of years behind them and not too many left and probably only this game to keep them going. It was somehow heartbreaking and uplifting at the same time.

So, there we were, back in paradise. This pool hall was my happy place. It had everything a man could want, pool, music, beer. Okay, no women, but it had everything else. There was even a snooker table, way at the back, which no one else ever seemed to use but which we always made a beeline straight for. I got the feeling that most of the guys in there didn't even know what it was - some foreigner's game, with way too many balls and way too much ground to cover. Will and I loved it though, we'd been playing for years. We'd first picked the game up in a pub in New Hampshire, a British-themed joint with the instructions written out in Old English on the placard hanging nearby. We'd spent an entire afternoon trying to wrap our heads round it, going over the legalese as if it were a set of Egyptian hieroglyphics to be guessed at and puzzled over and eventually deciphered. In the end we suspected we might have figured it out, but neither of us were a hundred percent sure. For all we knew, we were still doing the whole thing wrong.

"So how'd it go out there?" Will asked, bending over to take his shot.

"Not too well," I said.

Will had missed, it was my shot now. He wasn't as good at snooker as I was. Nor at pool, for that matter.

"Place didn't grab ya?"

"No, it didn't. Buncha fakeos and plastic shit. The beaches were nice though."

"I told you that was going to happen."
"You did?"
"Yeah."
"I don't remember that."
"I know, you were drunk."
Will finally put a red ball down and proceeded to lock horns with the black. You alternated red and other-colored, you see, that was how it worked. I drank half my beer down in one gulp, I was feeling good. Damn it was good to be back here again.

"So, how's it going with Priti?" I asked him.
"We broke up."
"*What*? How come you never tell me any of this shit?"
"You didn't ask."

He was being a smartass, which was to be expected, but he seemed tired as well, almost too tired to respond. Something I couldn't quite put my finger on, a certain weariness I'd never seen in him before. A lethargic haze. Early senility, perhaps. Then again, Will had always been slow-moving in general. Maybe it was only my imagination.

"Why'd you guys break up?"
"She wanted a commitment. You know how they get."

"'This horse shall never be tamed'," I said theatrically, quoting a line from one of his better songs.
"Indeed."
"You play any shows lately?"

"Nah, I've been cooling off with the music. Too much hassle for too little reward. You sit there playing for like three people and then get drunk, the same thing every night, I mean it kinda gets old."

"I know, I know. I don't know how you've kept doing it for as long as you have."
"How bout the writing? Finish your epic novel yet?"
"Hah. No progress whatsoever."
"That sucks."
"Yeah."

"You should write a story about two guys that go on a long bike tour of Philadelphia and then stop in to play snooker and drink beer all day long."

"And then what?"

"I dunno, the roof caves in or something. You're supposed to be the writer, you figure it out."

"I'm doing a novel though, that's enough for maybe five pages. Ten at most."

"I guess you're screwed then."

"What else is new."

Will missed a shot for about the hundredth time, then slowly toppled over and lay himself down face-first on the table. This was the usual routine with him, he beat his head against the wall for as long as he could and then gave up on life, he lay down on the table and refused to move. It was the signal that it was time to skedaddle and go looking for greener pastures. I knew from past experience that once he'd reached this point, there would be no way of coaxing another shot out of him, not a single one, no matter how hard I tried, even if I offered him a million dollars or more to do so. We handed the balls back in, said farewell to the rotund feller behind the counter and left. Goodbye for now, my paradise. Until we meet again.

So, the grand bike tour continued. We went here and there and cut down side streets and then all of a sudden the area wasn't looking so good anymore.

"You're taking me to the hood, aren't you," I said.

"Yes," Will said.

"Lovely."

"It's not that bad. There are far worse places around here, believe me."

We wound up at a nightclub in the black part of town. The sun had just gone down and it was cold, cold as a witch's tit, as a matter of fact. Will strikes again. He may have been a great guy but he had absolutely no common sense. We were going to freeze to death on the way back. If we didn't get mugged or shot first, that is.

We went inside to warm up. The place was packed with Saturday night revelers, with a line of drinkers at the long wooden bar and a teeming mass of twisting writhing bodies out on the dance floor. A band was playing, they weren't too bad. The singer was a middle-aged black dude with a mustache and a cute little hat on and a self-satisfied grin all over his face. It appeared he considered himself hot shit.

We squeezed in at one end and ordered beers. A hot black chick came over, wrapped in a tight white dress. She immediately grabbed ahold of Will and dragged him out onto the dance floor, almost before either of us even knew what was going on. I worked on my beer for a few minutes then turned around to see how he was faring. The two of them were in the middle of the dance floor; you could see Will from a mile away, his six-four (or five) frame sticking up above the rest like a skyscraper amongst lesser buildings. He was standing there bopping and jolting around. Will was a great musician but he was not a great dancer. That is to put it mildly; he was horrible. He was the worst dancer I'd ever seen. Will dancing conjured images of Frankenstein, he sort of lumbered around all herky-jerky with his arms out like he was coming to get you. The singer noticed and immediately spoke up.

"Get dat white boy outta dere! Somebody get dat white boy outta dere!" he was shouting into the microphone. He was doing this right in the middle of the song, he'd stopped singing to do it, it was crazy. Will was oblivious to the whole thing and just went right on dancing. The singer continued to steam, although he'd gone back to his singing at least. Finally, Will's escort brought him back over.

"What the hell was with that asshole," I said as the two of us chugged from bottles in tandem. I was madder than anyone else. "Do you believe the nerve of the guy?"

Will said nothing; I couldn't tell if he actually hadn't noticed what had happened, or if he was just embarrassed and was trying to hide it. A few people started coming over to tell Will how bad they felt for him, and what a complete jerk the singer had been. The little bastard's plan had failed – there he was, trying to puff himself up and make himself look cool, trying to keep his precious little social scene intact, all insular and untainted by goofy white boys and other assorted undesirables, and there the whole place was turning against him. People weren't always as shitty as you expected them to be, sometimes they surprised you. The guy actually had the gall to come over afterwards and talk to Will and me, not to apologize but to try to save face with the others. He patted Will on the back, no hard feelings, you know, and then went to shake my hand. I gave him my back and continued sucking on the bottle. No way was I shaking that hand, the little cunt could go throw himself off a cliff.

We went back outside just before last call. It was even colder now than before.

"Listen, Will, it's late and it's freezing cold and this isn't the greatest area anyway, what say we grab a cab? We can come back for the bikes tomorrow," I said.

"All right," Will said. He was usually pretty reasonable about stuff in general. Yet another reason to like the guy.

We went back and crashed, got up late the next morning and went down the street for coffee and donuts. The hangover had drained the color from both our faces, we looked like a pair of cadavers who'd somehow figured out how to walk. We didn't say much to each other as we sat there at the table eating and drinking, we didn't need to. Will and I were like family. We could sit there together in total silence like brothers and just enjoy each other's company. Sometimes I didn't know where I'd be if I had never met Will. All you needed was one friend really, one really good friend. Girlfriends and wives and big social circles were nice enough, I suppose, but in the end all you needed was that one friend and that was enough to get by.

39

A dream about Tracey. She's wrapped in my arms and we're kissing deeply, like we never did before, she isn't turning her face away like that night at her parents', only a few weeks before the big breakup. I've never felt anything like it; I'm uplifted, as in straight up to heaven. I feel whole. Her eyes are closed and her lips are parted and finally she's responding; she wants me, finally she wants me, the same way I want her.

The colors are shifting, all red and pink and gold, and through the haze I can see a little child, I can't tell if it's a boy or a girl, but whichever, the little child is walking down the street. Now I can see little pigtails bouncing, it's a girl, and she's skipping down the sidewalk, licking a lollipop as she goes, and the sun is out and it's a positively beautiful afternoon, the kind of afternoon that makes you glad to be alive. The kind of afternoon that comes along far more often when you're young. I'm watching the little girl bounce down the sidewalk and I'm expecting to find Tracey there at my side but when I turn my head to look she isn't there, either she never was or she's gone someplace else. I'm confused, I consider calling out for her, but

I don't, I just look around, wondering where she's gone. The little girl turns the corner just ahead of me while I'm distracted, and I run to catch up but now she's gone as well, she's disappeared from view, and now I'm casting about looking for answers trying to figure out what to do next and there's a ton of traffic in the road and I'm worried she's just gotten hit by a car and so I'm calling out for her, asking her to come back. Now to my dismay I can hear the sound of a child crying, sobbing somewhere off in the distance, but it's not the sound a six or seven-year-old would make, it's the crying of an infant, and once again I'm confused, I call out for Tracey but there's no answer, there's just this long wailing sob coming from somewhere in front of me.

I wake up with the sheets soaked through. I go into the bathroom to splash some water on my face and my hands are shaking so bad I can barely work the faucet. I go back and lay down. I lay there for an hour and of course there's no more sleep, just echoes from all that crying. I get up and get a glass of water, take it over and sit by the window. There are lots of clouds in the sky but every so often you can see stars.

40

So it was Lily that was on my mind now. That's right, Lily, the crazy chick from the bar, the one that had been singing and all the rest. To my surprise, she was still there. I went to her apartment and knocked on the door one afternoon, and lo and behold, Lily answered the door. I couldn't believe it, I figured she would have moved on or been committed or died or something by now.

She looked both surprised and delighted. She invited me in.

"I was wondering when I'd see you again... Where the hell'd you run off to?"

"California."

"What the hell were you doing in California?"

"I don't know."

She laughed, a bright chirping noise. She was at least half bird. She lit up a cigarette and then went into the kitchen to get drinks. She re-emerged with two cans, threw one in my lap and plopped herself down next to me on the couch. We talked for a while and things moved along lightly and breezily and it was nice, all was well. I began to revise my original assessment, that there'd been something wrong with her. There was actually nothing wrong with her at all. The possibility existed that I was too judgmental. I'd been told that before.

The following afternoon I was back over at her place. It was a Sunday and a light snow was falling, and we were looking for something to do. Lily was all fired up, she was wearing some crazy hat with feathers sticking out of it, at all sorts of strange angles. She was definitely an odd chick. There I was, being judgmental again. Okay: she was a free spirit. How's that.

"Oh, I just love it when the snow falls!" she was exclaiming as we walked out onto the stoop and she was closing the door behind us. "Don't you?"

She jumped up in the air like a little kid, then went around trying to catch the snowflakes on her tongue. We'd decided to go to a bar. As aforementioned, there was nothing else to do in the world. Especially when the weather was cold.

So we went to a place just around the corner, a local hangout Lily was evidently quite well familiar with. The bartender was as old as the hills, he looked like he dated back to the Revolutionary War. I thought about asking him how George was doing. He moved pretty well for an old codger though, he shuffled around at a decent speed and poured pints like it was no problem at all. I hoped I'd be as operational when I got to that age.

"The snow is falling, Marv! Isn't it wonderful?"

"It is, Lily, it is," he chuckled. He appeared well acquainted with her antics.

Suddenly she threw her arms around me and gave me a big wet kiss. "It's great to see you again," she whispered in my ear. I told her the feeling was mutual.

We spent the rest of the afternoon there at the bar, and some of the evening as well. One of Lily's friends came in and we shot the breeze, some young kid who was down on his luck, trying to find a job and meeting with no success. When we got tired of drinking beer we went out and got tacos. Life felt normal for the first time in quite some time. A sign of things to come, perhaps.

41

I was back at my parents' place, doing the whole dinner engagement thing. It wasn't steak this time, it was something else. I think she'd said pork. It was happy hour and we were sitting in the living room, jousting.

"So, I take it you've gotten all this California stuff out of your system?" my Dad said.

I didn't appreciate the sarcasm. It wasn't quite a wise crack but it was close. I didn't take the bait, I said nothing.

"Have you given any more thought about getting that new car?" he asked.

"Plenty. I think about it all day long. I sit around thinking about it to the exclusion of all else. It's pretty much all I can think about."

One smartass deserved another. Now it was his turn to go quiet, and a little red. My mother jumped in to steer us toward calmer waters.

"What's new, Jim? Any new developments?" she asked.

"I have a girlfriend," I said, airily.

"You have *what*? Why didn't you tell me? Who is she, where did you meet her, what's she like? I can't believe you didn't tell me, Jimmy."

"Her name is Lily. I met her in a bar. She's nice."

My mother pressed me for more details for a while, I gave her one or two and then it was time for dinner. We ate in relative silence, just the sound of clinking cutlery and not much else. My parents seemed older now, still arrogant as all hell but more mellow, more muted and restrained. Faded, was the word that came to mind. I guess they were just getting old. And in spite of the wise cracks, I was finding the conversation a little easier to bear than in days of old - I couldn't say I related to them exactly, but it was closer than it had been before. I must have been getting old myself.

When dinner was over, we went down into the family room to watch some television. My Dad lay himself down in his customary corner and was soon fast asleep, slipping ever deeper into the folds of the couch and snoring away like a locomotive. I asked Mom how Jake was doing and she said not too well, it wasn't good news. She said he was as gloomy and withdrawn as ever and was once again refusing to speak with anyone. I'd been meaning to go over there for ages but for some reason I'd been procrastinating, and now after getting the status update from my mother I was feeling guilty about not having done it sooner. I guess I was worried about what I'd find there, that seeing him still mired in that same tortured malaise he'd been in previously would be more than a little upsetting. But I was going to have to do it, there really wasn't a choice, I'd have to get my ass over there and see how Jake was doing, and if what my mother was saying was true then it would have to be sooner rather than later. I mean I was his brother, after all. That's what brothers were for. I think I'd read that somewhere once. Jake was a disgruntled little bastard and a real pain in the ass when he wanted to be, but it sounded like he really needed some help this time. He was way too proud to ever ask for it, so I'd just have to go over there and give him some, whether he liked it or not. I'd go this week, no more dallying, no more screwing around. I'd go over and see Jake this week. Friday at the latest.

42

I went over on Friday, after work. I found the right address and knocked on the door. No one answered but I could see someone moving around in there, through the little window in front.

"Come on Jake, let me in. Open up the door."

The commotion inside had stopped, now he was hiding.

"Come on, Jake. I just want to talk."

I tried knocking again, I tried pounding on the door, I yelled, I cajoled, I pleaded, but nothing worked. I thought about breaking the door down. After about ten minutes I gave up and went back down the street. He really didn't want to talk to anyone.

That night I got a call from Craig, he was down in Florida now. He and Lizzy had broken up.

"Hey, I'm dancin' in a strip club now!"

"What?"

"Yeah, it's a gay place. I get up on stage a couple times a night and shake my ass and they come up and stick dollar bills in my shorts, it's pretty wild."

I didn't ask if that meant he was gay or not. I assumed the answer was yes. Then again, you never knew with that guy, maybe he was just doing it for the experience, to amuse himself, just for something to do. He went on at length about dancing at the gay place, he said he was making good money, that everyone there treated him real nice, that they paid all sorts of attention to him. It sounded like he'd found some sort of niche for himself. Then he hit me with it.

"I was thinking about going up north, maybe stay with you a while. Whaddya think?"

Images of street fights and lines of coke and naked chicks at the door came firmly into view. I considered it another five seconds further and then decided to deflect. Too risky. He was going to get me either killed or thrown in jail, and I was too old for that shit. I mumbled some lame excuse about being better on my own, a lone wolf, you know how it is; Craig sounded disappointed but didn't protest too much. When I got off the phone with him, I felt relieved. I didn't know if I'd ever been high-speed enough to keep up that kind of pace. Probably not. I had more of my father in me than even I knew.

So, the days passed. The job went on and on. I was spending a lot of time with Lily, at night and on weekends and as time permitted. She was indeed crazy, but in a good way, full of a different sort of life than I'd ever encountered before – she danced around all the time, sung whenever the mood struck, said whatever was on her mind, regardless of the situation or whoever happened to be around. It was alternately refreshing and exhausting, depending on how much energy I had.

Every now and then I'd sit down at the desk and try to write, but the words were flowing slower than ever. They weren't just non-immortal now, they were nonexistent. Over time the stints grew less and less frequent, to the point where I finally had to admit to myself that I was basically giving up. It was too hard, it just wasn't working. Maybe I wasn't meant to be a writer at all. Maybe I was supposed to be a male stripper too, who knew. Maybe I'd revisit the novel again someday, but the way I felt right now, I was pretty much done with it.

And I wasn't the only one. I was sensing from Will that he was slowing down with the music as well. He had recorded an album on his own a while back (a damn fine album at that) and the last I'd heard he was giving the last few copies away to the record stores, just throwing them into the record bins and forgetting about it, just throwing them away.

Life was too sad for words. They gave you all these hopes and dreams at the beginning just to squash them like bugs at the end. It was almost like they were doing it on purpose. Sadistic little fuckers, they were.

43

I was back in Philly, visiting Will. He was supposedly dating some hippie chick now and we were all going to hang out. We swung by her apartment to pick her up; it was a rickety old place hanging from the side of a building, with crazy wooden staircases running up to the door and curtains hanging all over everything inside, like some kind of commune. She had a roommate in there somewhere, some guy named Jeff who was something of a weirdo, or so Will had told me. Anyway, we scooped Megan up (Megan, that was her name) and whisked her off with us. I'd like to be able to tell you we went somewhere other than a bar, but I'd be lying if I did. We made right for the nearest watering hole and installed ourselves on the stools provided, prepared to imbibe at will. Megan was spaced out, with a dreamy stare that was permanently off somewhere in an adjacent galaxy. They were all spaced out, Will and all his girlfriends and everyone else for that matter. It was a world full of astronauts. Megan and I talked between sips of beer and got to know one another a little bit.

She was another big walker, she liked to walk as much as Will did, she walked to and from work five miles a day. I tried getting a look at her legs; they must have been like a marathon runner's.

"So, what do you think of her?" Will asked during a break in the action.

"I like her. But then again I liked Priti too."

"You should be able to have more than one girlfriend."

"There's this place called Utah; you should check it out. I think you'd like it."

I hadn't told him about Lily yet, and I wasn't sure why. My own mind was oftentimes a mystery to me. Megan was a good-looking girl, blonde-haired and blue-eyed, small and thin and mousy, although I hadn't known that beforehand. Still, there might have been ulterior motives involved.

"Where did you go to school?" I asked Megan.

"I didn't go to college. I was home-schooled as a kid."

"Wow, I've never met anyone who was home-schooled." It was true, I hadn't. "How come you didn't go to regular school?"

"Because the kids bullied me too much."

There was a pain in her eyes as she said it, a real flash of soul. Another flawed gem Will had unearthed, another diamond in the rough. I didn't know where he found them.

I turned back to Will. "I like her," I repeated.

We went barhopping for a few more hours and then wound up at a real swinging place, one of the bigger productions, with the big open room and a million tables and people running around everywhere. We got a booth along the wall and ordered food. I got fish and chips, which I hadn't ordered in about a million years. Megan had a salad; she was one of these chicks that ate like a bird. Will had gone strangely quiet and I began to realize he was drunk already, he'd been hitting it unusually hard that night for some reason. Megan and I cozied up to each other and we got progressively more friendly. She was quite drunk and I was well on the way; I accelerated my efforts, ordered another pitcher of beer. The party spun on, midnight came and went. Will was now crumpled in the corner, either passed out or asleep or somewhere in between. Megan and I did some more quiet chatting there in the cramped confines of the booth and then our eyes met and something happened, there was recognition, a mutual spark of interest, something entirely unexpected and intensely exciting. Suddenly she was putting the beers down like there was no tomorrow and I was following suit just to keep up and then the next thing I knew the three of us were stumbling out into the street and trying to hail a cab. We found one, piled in and a few minutes later were at Will's front door. He was practically comatose, all but out on his feet, it took him about three minutes to get the key in the lock. We fell inside as one, and then Will fell down on the floor, went down like a tree face-first and just lay there, sprawled out like a dead praying mantis. I gathered him up as best I could and dragged him into his bedroom, threw him down on the bed and then when I turned around Megan was standing there behind me. I didn't need to think twice, didn't need to ask, didn't need to do anything at all, she just wound up in my arms and then our lips were locked and our hands were running up and down each other's bodies, a big questing quivering mass of arousal about to topple over onto the bed, right on top of Will's prone form. My god, her body felt good, so thin and lithe, so warm and smooth, so soft and yielding and utterly feminine. Women were the original miracle, there was practically no second place. A night like this came along once in a blue moon, when everything clicked, everything finally worked, and it made you want to live forever, made all the other shit worth the effort. A smidgen of my sentient self was trying to feel guilty about what I was doing, considering I already had a girlfriend and my best friend's new girlfriend was in fact the one currently wrapped up in my arms, but I was too drunk to care. That, and screw it anyway, you only lived once. Maybe that made me some kind of asshole. Fine, so be it, I was an asshole. Most of the others appeared to be assholes as well, I was certainly in good company. Megan and I embraced for a few fleeting seconds more before prudence finally got the better of her and she pulled away. She collapsed on the bed in a beautiful blonde heap and I went into the living room to lay down on the couch. It had been one of the more interesting nights in recent memory. We all needed more like this.

Megan went home the following morning, she had something to do that day. She said it had been very nice to meet me, and I said the feeling was mutual, and very much meant it.

"Wow, what a girl," I enthused over coffee.

"Meh, I don't know."

"Are you crazy? You're gonna let that one get away too?"

"There's something missing. She feels like my sister or something."

"Do you always hook up with your sisters?"

"Only occasionally. I try not to make a habit of it."

"Inbreeding and such."

"Correct." He threw his napkin down. "Come, we must be off 'fore the advent of midday." There, he'd come out of his funk; finally, he was starting to sound like himself again.

"You wanna do some more biking?" he asked.

"No more bikes, please," I said with a sigh. The last bike he'd had me on had just about disemboweled me. I didn't see how anyone could have children after tangling with a contraption like that.

"The feet it shall be, then," he announced.

It being too early to drink, we found a park and sat ourselves down in it. It was a big wide-open space, with a few other people scattered around in the grass, picnicking and lounging around, just wasting time like us.

"How's the music going?" I asked him.

"Almost dead. Barely even thinking about it these days. How's the writing?"

"Same. Can't do it no mo'. It takes years off my life every time I even try."

"None of it matters. We'll all be dead soon."

I'd been looking the other way when he'd said it; I glanced over to see if he was serious, but he was grinning, he'd meant it in jest. Or had he.

"Don't get me down, I got enough problems as it is."

"Suck it up. Don't be a pussy."

It was my line, the one I usually used to goad him into doing something, he'd stolen it. Another grin, he was feeling playful.

We had lunch, we had more coffee, we stopped for a couple of leisurely afternoon beers. Day drinking was fun, it always felt like doing something naughty. Then the sun was going down and it was time for the final act - we were going back over to the neighborhood tavern place to pay a visit to Oleg, the drunken Polish bartender, the one with the Lithuanian buddy. We were in for a disappointment though, because when we got there it was closed, as in permanently, it was all boarded up.

"Well, I'll be damned," Will said, shaking his head. "It had been a long time coming, he'd been talking about closing down for years."

My heart sank. Places like this were in short supply these days; the world needed more of them, not less. The good old-fashioned dive bars were going under in droves and all that remained were the fancy nightclubs and the goddamn martini bars and all the rest of that yuppified living death. People were too stupid for words.

The closure of an institution had taken the wind out of our sails. We limped along to the next place for a nightcap but it was an entirely listless affair. I thought about Oleg and the Lithuanian, and the great time we'd had there only a few months before. Those times would never be possible again. It was like they'd scalloped out another little scoopful of life and tossed it aside, broken off another little piece and thrown it on the fire, like so much kindling. Bastardos. Stop ruining the planet. There are few enough places left to go without you shrinking the pool even further. Stick to your goddamn fancy-ass hotel bars and chic restaurants and leave the rest of us alone. Leave us at least one hole to drown our sorrows in.

Will and I went home, almost sober for once. I couldn't tell if it was a good or bad thing, if it were a sign of nascent maturity or one of impending spiritual demise. In any event, we were getting old, there was no doubt about it. You could fend it off for as long as you could, you could keep pretending you were still a kid and that everything still impressed you and set you on fire the same way it had before, back at the beginning of time when the light was still in your eyes and you thrilled to every sight and loved everyone and everything the same, but you were just kidding yourself. The lights went out at their own pace, and once they did they were out forever.

44

Jake still wasn't seeing anyone. My parents were getting worried, they sent me back over there to try again but it was just the same thing. Then I got the call, he'd tried to kill himself, he'd taken a whole bunch of pills. I went to the hospital and met my parents in the waiting area. When my mother saw me, she came over and threw her arms around me, sobbing hysterically, asking why he'd done it, over and over, why had he done it. My father stood nearby, looking as grim and imperturbable as always. I was sure it was bothering the hell out of him but he was determined not to let on, not to fall to pieces in a public place. He was trying to stay strong for my mother. My Dad wasn't a bad guy, he was just confused.

We sat in chairs until the doctor came to see us. He told us Jake was going to be all right but we wouldn't be able to visit him for a couple of days. His system was a mess and he was still very weak. The doctor went away and my parents and I sat back down. I wasn't sure if I should talk or not.

"How'd they find him?" I asked tentatively. I figured I might get scolded for my efforts but the response that came back was quite gentle.

"The neighbors downstairs heard noises. They said he'd been yelling, and then they heard a thump on the floor," my mother said. My father was shaking his head, he looked like he was still in disbelief.

"What are we going to do," my mother moaned, putting her head in her hands.

I didn't know, I couldn't offer any advice. We stayed a little while longer and then went home. Back at the house, Mom brewed a pot of coffee and we all drank some. Mom had called her sister Erica and she was supposed to be coming over later, just to offer some support, to be with the family in their time of need, all that sort of thing. I stayed long enough to keep up appearances and then left. I didn't want to be there. I went back to the apartment and stayed up half the night, steaming. It was making me mad now; if he'd felt that bad then why hadn't he just said something, why hadn't he let me in. God damn it, I didn't understand people. And yet again, I did. I'd had moments as dark as Jake had, or at least close to it, and I knew full well how hard it could be to find anyone to really understand. When you were in a hole that deep, it was all but impossible to show anyone around you just how deep and dark it was, it was an inconceivable state of affairs unless you were the one mired in it. You were alone in a sea of thousands. I pictured Jake in my mind, how he'd looked as a kid, how he looked now, how much he'd changed. It was too much, it overwhelmed me; I drank my beers down, I paced the room, I bit my fist until blood poured down, until the tears were pouring down as well. He was my brother, he was my own flesh and blood and there was nothing I could do for him. I couldn't accept the thought.

45

Jake recovered and went to live with my parents. They kept him in the hospital for a week, some people wanted to ask him some questions, about how he felt and if he was going to be all right. The men in the white coats and all that. It appeared he'd passed the test.

Life went on. I went to work, I came home from work. I drank beer by myself in that shitty little apartment out in the middle of nowhere. Things had cooled off with Lily and I hadn't heard from Will in a while. I was back in a bad spot, the old familiar place. There was nothing to do, no one to see, nowhere to go. At least not around here. I went into the city a couple of times and went roaming around but that didn't help matters any, all I did was get drunk. I was lost. We all were.

One day I woke up and instead of going to work, I didn't. I didn't call in sick, I didn't make coffee, I didn't do anything at all, I just sat on the couch for a good three hours or so. I couldn't do it anymore. And even if I could, I wasn't going to. I was stopping, that was it. I'd had enough.

I went into the bedroom, dragged the beat-up old suitcase out from under the bed and threw about two weeks' worth of clothes in there, whatever would fit. I took the suitcase and went outside and tossed it in the trunk, went back and locked the door. Then I got in the car and drove away. The utility bills were coming due in a couple of days, I wondered how long it would take for them to shut the power off.

www.ingramcontent.com/pod-product-compliance
Lightning Source LLC
Chambersburg PA
CBHW061216210726
48294CB00006B/1865